PRAISE FOR *FLYING CARPETS*

"Hedy Habra's *Flying Carpets* is an enchanting collection of short stories... Each story takes the reader on a magical flight spurred on by longing, loss, and the search for the intangible yet true... Habra's thoughtful tone, insightful imagination, and cosmopolitan grace infuse her stories with lightness tinged with gravitas, giving her narratives a mysterious quality that lingers in the reader's mind long after her stories end."

—Al-Jadid

"Hedy Habra's *Flying Carpets* is a collection of enchantments and wonders charmingly recounted, deeply imagined, and composed with lyrical exactitude. It belongs to that rare tradition of books whose spells grow increasingly seductive with each new story."

—Stuart Dybek, author of *Coast of Chicago* and *Sailing with Magellan*

"Hedy Habra's moving, lovely stories emerge from her history as a Middle Eastern writer exposed to the varied cultures of Egypt, Lebanon, Belgium, Greece, and the United States, fluent in French, Arabic, Spanish and English. She draws together in this volume vivid images, events, and voices in a compelling, parti-colored vision that evokes time and place like the haunting recollections from a dream."

—Arnold Johnston, author of *The Witching Voice: A Novel from the Life of Robert Burns* and *What the Earth Taught Us* (poems)

FLYING CARPETS

by Hedy Habra

Interlink Books

An imprint of Interlink Publishing Group, Inc.
Northampton, Massachusetts

First published in 2013 by
INTERLINK BOOKS
An imprint of Interlink Publishing Group, Inc.
46 Crosby Street, Northampton, Massachusetts 01060
www.interlinkbooks.com

Some of the stories in *Flying Carpets* have appeared—sometimes in slightly different versions—in the following publications: *Dinarzad's Children: An Anthology of Arab American Fiction* (2nd ed.): "Distances" and "Mariam" (2009); *Dream International Quarterly*: "Tell me, Mayra" (1997); *GraFemas: Letras Femeninas*: Victoria Urbino Prize "Noor El Qamar" (2007); *Linden Lane Magazine*: "They Won't Miss me this Afternoon," "Flight," and "Succession" (1991); *Linden Lane Magazine*: "Search," "Ducks Flight," and "Shuffling Seasons" (1993); *Linden Lane Magazine*: "The Green Book" (1992); *Luciole Press*: "The Mantis" (2011); *Mizna Literary Journal*: "Green Figs and Cherries" (2008); *Parting Gifts: Qedeshim Qedeshot*: "The Flood" (2010) and "*Al Kasdir*" (2011); *Rockhurst Review*: "The Fisherman" (2008); *The Saranac Review*: "By Fire or Water" (2011). *The Smoking Poet*: "12 Rushdy Street" (2011).

Recognitions and awards: *Letras Femeninas AILFCH*: Victoria Urbano Literary Contest "Noor el Qamar" (First Prize) (2007); *New Voices* Contest: "Anemone's Fingers" Honorable Mention (1992); *New Voices* Contest: "Mariam" Honorable Mention (1993).

Library of Congress Cataloging-in-Publication Data
Habra, Hedy.
[Short stories. Selections]
Flying Carpets / by Hedy Habra. -- First edition.
    pages cm
ISBN 978-1-56656-957-6
1. Storytelling--Fiction. I. Title.
PS3608.A2455F59 2013
813'.6--dc23
                          2013023661

Printed and bound in the United States of America

TABLE OF CONTENTS

I

AL KASDIR

When I was ten years old I used to accompany my mother everywhere, especially during the long summer vacations. We would go to the Heliopolis Sporting Club, to the movies or visit friends and relatives. We favored going to my aunt Sophie's, whose balcony overlooked the Oasis, an open-air cinema that featured a great number of Italian and Indian productions. While adults were chatting inside over tea and pastries, my cousins and I would watch movies converted from afar into quasi-silent functions, especially when we couldn't read the subtitles and lovers were whispering.

I remember one day in particular at my aunt's house. That's when I had the privilege to witness a *Kasdir* ritualistic session, a far more exciting spectacle than anything ever projected on the Oasis' large screen. Why was I the only child present? I'm not sure anymore. Maybe my cousin Monique's sons had already left for the club with their nanny.

What I am certain of is that we arrived late afternoon when the women had just finished their manicure. Of my aunt's five children, only one still lived at home, Denise, a thirty-year-old single woman. Her older sister Monique, recently widowed at thirty-five, spent most of her free time with them. The manicurist, Salma, who usually came monthly to prepare *halawa*—a sweet sticky concoction used to rid women of all unwanted body hair—was scheduled every other week for the manicure and pedicure. But Salma had other talents, which she promised to demonstrate as soon as the nails would dry. She had divination powers. I drank my lemonade on the balcony overlooking the cinema. From that third floor, several rows of seats were visible across the street lined with tall Eucalyptus trees, whose lower foliage was not dense enough to hide the entire screen, only some edges.

The day I witnessed the *Kasdir* ceremony there was mystery in the air. Smiles and whispers piqued my curiosity. I sensed that something special was going to take place so I returned to the sitting room where the women were chatting. They were waving their hands in the air, delicately edged with long oval-shaped enameled nails. I envied their petalled fingertips because mine were bitten to the bone. The manicurist was neatly packing the tools of her trade in a wooden rectangular sewing basket, aligning clippers, files and scissors in their compartments and nail polish bottles in the lower case, then securing them with folded hand towels. I think now she was taking her time, meditating as she was getting ready to delve into the role of soothsayer about to predict Denise's and Monique's future.

Zeinab, the maid, brought cups, a large bowl full of cold water and a couple of towels. She placed a Primus kerosene burner on the Formica table that served for the manicure. It was needed to melt *al kasdir*, the gray tin that was central to the divination process. Salma asked Zeinab to fetch a radio.

"Do you want to play music," asked my mother?

Zeinab and Salma answered with a same voice: "No, we need to put the prayers on." They explained that it was indispensable for the reading session.

"No," objected my aunt. She mumbled that it was nonsense, mixing religion with fortune-telling, "This part we'll skip . . ."

But they all stopped her: "No big deal. It's OK; let's go on with it. We aren't serious about this! It's just for fun!"

Once the incantations were heard in the background, Salma warned them to concentrate upon their own wishes and desires. She asked Denise to bend her head slightly and covered it with one of the towels for protection. Salma placed the bowl filled with water on top of her head and made sure Zeinab was holding on to it with both hands. Using tongs, Salma seized pieces of tin from a small metallic cup she had placed over the Primus' bluish flame. Then in a sleight of hand, she bent both tongs and flame right over the bowl. From the softened tin, a molten gray substance dripped with a hissing sound into the cold water, acquiring strange shapes, opening up like flowers or ruffled mushrooms. Salma contemplated these floating solidified shapes for a while, gathered them with tongs as she removed the bowl from Denise's head, saying, "Look carefully: there is someone seriously interested in you. He will come next week right here, to your house. He is older than you but attractive and distinguished. He has money. You have met him before."

Monique shrugged: "That's it, I don't want to do this. Anyway who would want to marry a widow? Penniless and with children! Let's be real, I don't believe in all of this. If Denise has met the guy before then what's the point of seeing it in *al kasdir*?"

They all protested, talking at the same time: "Come on, let's do it! *Yallah!* None of us really believes in this but let us get it over with! We've been waiting long enough for Salma to do what she promised. Be a good sport, let's see what your luck is." Aunt Sophie was laughing and crying at the same time, wiping off the tears from her cheeks. She knew that whoever might come to visit Denise would be discouraged right away. Denise's bad temper and directness were hard to take. Finally, Monique was convinced to submit to the experiment, although she was right: even though she was charming and sweet, it was very hard in those times for a widow with two children to find a husband unless she were rich. Her husband, who was a successful businessman, died of a heart attack before being able to make provisions for the family.

Such situations were at the root of my decision to go to the university later on and fend for myself. Surrounded with helpless widows, in a culture in which they were supposed to be protected by either a father or a husband, I knew I needed to become a professional and have something solid to fall back upon in case my future husband would pass away. I never thought of divorcing though. In retrospect I realize that nowadays women think of the eventuality of a divorce before that one of becoming a widow, but in those days that was never an option since there was no civil marriage. We were Catholics: no one divorced and that was the end of it. All that women around me could wish for was a prospect of marriage, always a solution brought along by a man. . . . I understood why Monique found it ridiculous to resort to *al kasdir,* even playfully, to solve her future. Salma melted another piece of tin in the bowl held over Monique's head, listening carefully to the rustling sounds of the metallic drops bursting as if trying to escape drowning. She frowned as she observed the wrinkled, distorted forms that were allotted to her: "Hum. . . . " She seemed reluctant to speak for a while, then said that the reading wasn't always accurate, that it should be repeated at another time.

"But what's the matter?" Monique worried. "Are you seeing anything bad? Tell me. I want to know."

Salma smiled. "No, there is nothing to worry about. Nothing. That's the problem. I see nothing coming your way, no men, no suitors no prospects of marrying again. But remember, this is just for now. We will have to do it all over again."

At this point, I was beginning to feel bored and wanted to go home.

I was trying to get my mother's attention and tell her it was time to leave but by then they were all adamant she should participate in the ritual. The best part was watching my cousins and aunt trying to convince her to let Salma read *al kasdir* one last time. She refused categorically: "I don't want a husband! I won't sacrifice my children. Don't you know a stepfather never cares for his wife's children? Always wants kids of his own and becomes jealous of a mother's attentions to her children. No way! I dedicated myself to my three children: they are my life. Besides I won't ever find anyone like my Johnny." My father had died over a year before of a heart attack, leaving her in her early forties with responsibilities she had never been prepared to fulfill. It was hard to see her struggle daily with the succession, the bureaucracy and endless paperwork. She had to go several times a week to Cairo and wait in line in government buildings to retrieve the required documents and try to take care of my father's affairs. But that day I could sense she was playful and deep inside wanted to have her luck read.

"Henriette, it's your turn," they said. "It's getting late. Salma has to go." And she did comply, pretending she was really doing it for their sake. But I could tell she was having fun and even believed a little in Salma's powers.

By now I was becoming very interested in Salma's reading. She seemed to do everything faster the third time around. Her face beamed as she bent her head and listened to the snakelike hissing sounds whispering in her ear. She then paused, looking really pleased as she meditated over the strange tin efflorescence that resurfaced on my mother's behalf. Salma declared that my mother's luck was greater than the two younger women's and that she was going to remarry very soon because more than one man were on their way to her house. She even assured her: "There is a man, I can see him distinctly who has not forgotten you for decades. He will soon come closer to you!" A heavy silence followed her words. We were all stunned at such affirmations and no one questioned Salma's words. My aunt seemed preoccupied all of a sudden and my mother's expression became stern as she told me, "It's getting late, we should take care of dinner. Time to go." Suddenly, each of them was thinking aloud of what they had to do next while Zeinab and Salma were cleaning up and disappeared towards the kitchen.

We returned home after doing some errands. I often wondered what went wrong because I never heard the *Kasdir* mentioned since. "But what of the readings," I often thought to myself, "were they at all accurate?" Maybe there was a tacit decision to forget this episode. Over the years it did occur to me to find out if any of these predictions came close when I'd hear of a potential suitor for Denise and Monique. But whenever I'd refer to *al kasdir*, everybody changed the subject.

My aunt's house became associated with the fleeting scenes of the foreign movies we watched from her balcony, and I could never make a connection between anyone's love life and the tin's configurations.

* * *

Something happened at one point several years later that brought back the *Kasdir* to the forefront. I was preparing my Baccalaureate and was spending most of my time at home, studying. One afternoon, I overheard an exceptionally loud conversation in the living room where my mother was entertaining some friends for tea. My grandmother was arguing vehemently and I decided to join them to find out what had managed to get my gentle Nonna to raise her voice, "*Basta! Basta,* Henriette! Why don't you get over it! This is all fantasy!"

It was common knowledge that my mother was never allowed to marry her first love. Shortly after agreeing to their union, her family forced her to break their two-months-long engagement under the pretext that the young man would never have a substantial career that would enable him to meet her needs. Heart broken, the young fiancés were not to meet again except for one last visit in a church, chaperoned by her mother. I knew of this story, of course. My mother kept repeating it, without omitting a single detail, especially after my father's death. She often stressed that this man had remained single for several years. It was when she decided to accept my father that he finally tied the knot.

The novelty at the heart of the discussion at teatime was that this respectable family man had just passed away. But before dying, he had confessed to his sister Odette—who was my mother's childhood friend—that he had never forgotten his first love and insisted that she would be told. Exultant, moved or just excited—this much I will never know—my mother burst victoriously, "Can't you see? This was all predicted by Salma years ago! *Al kasdir* never fails." She looked around her with conviction, "How many times didn't we all witness it?" I couldn't believe what came next. Apparently, a few years before Salma's reading, mother's former suitor was widowed. He had even tried to get in touch with her. That's when she convinced my father to withdraw from certain social circles. Her friend Alice interjected, "Don't forget that after Johnny died, he sent word with Odette that he was seriously interested in you."

"What do you expect, Alice! I wasn't going to bring a step-father home!" She rolled her eyes, then added sententiously, "But in the end, we all agree that *al kasdir* works!"

"*Bass, Bass! Basta!*" My grandmother frowned, pursing her lips in reproval. A pious woman, she was deeply offended by this attitude while all the other women present sided with my mother. That was the last time I heard them arguing about the subject. I left for Beirut that summer to pursue graduate studies and Nonna passed away a year later. My mother joined me soon after and from then on I would often hear her recall the *Kasdir* sessions when we had company, openly stating how soundly she believed in them, and what a pity Salma wasn't around to prove it.

THE GREEN BOOK
a *catherinette*'s diary

But, let me tell you. A French tradition has it that if a girl isn't married at twenty-five, she is said to have worn St. Catherine's headdress. It was about time she found a husband. When we were still schoolgirls, we used to laugh at twenty-five-year-old single girls calling them *catherinettes*. It was impossible to forget that St. Catherine's day fell on the 25th of November. That was when our school held its annual charity Kermess, named after the saint. Ours was a French nuns' school, Pensionnat de la Mère de Dieu, located in Garden City, one of Cairo's loveliest suburbs bordering the Nile. Those were the bygone days of king Farouk's apogee, and believe me, Cairo had nothing to envy to the most dazzling European capitals. Yet, anyway, not much has changed regarding marriage, I assure you.

After I reached the fatidic age, it must have been around the mid thirties, or rather around 1937 to be more accurate, I tried not to attach importance to what young people today would consider a trifle. Yet, the following couple of years, I avoided going to the Kermess.

When Emile proposed, I was inclined to consider him more seriously than any other before him. My parents tried to influence me every time a possible match came along. "Yvonne, you'll never make up your mind. Look around you. Your friends' children are growing. Don't wait too long." They urged me to accept Emile: "You're lucky at your age to find such a good man. He comes from a respectable family. He has a comfortable, solid situation." My mother added, "He'll give you security and a family. He's crazy about you. What more do you want?"

"He is much older," I objected.

"Fifteen years is not a big deal," said my father. "He's good looking, athletic. Women age much faster than men; you'll always look young by his side. He'll be faithful. Believe me."

* * *

Emile was very much in love, and faithful. But he demanded to be in control of everything. I had to explain every minute detail. Every single expense had to be recorded: taxis, hairdresser, tips, tramways, food, and clothes. When the children came it got more and more complicated. At the same time, however, I discovered a stratagem that allowed us to live in peace.

From the very beginning, Emile asked me to keep a written record of the household's expenses. I'd spend hours, writing, bent over the huge multi-colored Spanish shawl spread over our dining-room table. I'd push aside the long silky fringes, place a thick gray cotton pad over a corner of the lacquered mahogany, careful not to damage the table's shiny finish with an ink stain. First, I noted all the figures in pencil. Then, in my green book,

I wrote the day's date in red on top of the page and the list of items with their prices in black.

I had a variety of different sized pens that I kept in an old rectangular jewelry box. The gold and silver pens were arranged over the red velvet lining according to their shape. The box was deep enough to fit the ink bottles and the pen holder. I firmly inserted the chosen pen into the wooden holder and dipped it in red or black ink. I used an incredible amount of blotting paper then. But I refused to use a modern fountain pen. This way, the result was more elegant.

Back in school I'd always won first prize in calligraphy. I had also sewed, you know, embroidered, crocheted, and painted. The Mother Superior used to tell me with a tap on the shoulder, "Child, you put beauty in everything you touch." I started two recipe books at fifteen. All the titles were in red Gothic script and the rest in black cursive. Over two years I recorded friends' and relatives' recipes on long rectangular loose-leafs; then I bound them with black linen and leather hardcover. I added a drawing at the bottom of each page as a visual memento of the dish or dessert. Drawing was to me a natural extension of writing; this is why I loved calligraphy. I liked to form the letters, align them across the page, and shape them with a twist of the hand and with sensitive strokes into black or red signs. In the process, I'd lose track of their meaning. Some letters resembled hieroglyphs, others were ornate like a baroque cathedral.

Keeping a book was not a chore, after all. I grew accustomed to my green book. It even gave me a real sense of power. With time, Emile trusted me and only routinely checked the accounts. He let me manage the servants and make all the domestic decisions. He only worried when I asked for more money. He used to say, "Yvonne, is it for something we really need?"

"Well," I'd answer, "but of course! It's all relative. I realize that."

It isn't that he wasn't generous. He just needed to be convinced of the necessity of the purchase. "I want you and the children to have the best," he often repeated, "but we have to be reasonable. We can't throw money out the window."

Sometimes we argued for hours over money, never reaching an agreement. It was the same when we talked about politics, love, or religion: The three things my grandfather always advised to avoid socially. Emile loved to go to the movies, but our views were so different that we would end up fighting instead of exchanging opinions. I finally understood that the age gap could not be bridged and gradually tried to elude discussions. The fewer words exchanged, the happier we were.

Emile used to come home from work eager to talk about his day for a while: "We're going to need a new employee. Raymond is doing a lot of traveling now, and I can't deal on my own with the customers during his absence." I'd listen without making any comment. His business was growing. He and his partner, Raymond, owned a store downtown in Midan Suleyman Pasha. They sold fabric for men's suits and coats and took turns going to London and Paris to order their merchandise. Everything in Emile's life went according to his plans. He was content and told everyone how lucky he was. His wife, Yvonne, was such a good cook, so skilled in everything. A real pearl. And Yvonne this, and Yvonne that.

After the children were born, our standard of living grew along with the expenses. Emile was confident of my efficiency and although he only looked at my green book occasionally, I kept it faithfully. I had discovered a new pleasure. I could play around with the figures without him ever noticing. When I'd buy school supplies, I'd mark ten books instead of the eight required, four uniforms instead of two. When I'd buy the children's clothes, I'd automatically add a pair of pajamas, half a dozen pieces of underwear, or socks. In my green book, the market prices fluctuated arbitrarily according to my pen's whimsy. As a result, I always had some pocket money. I could buy things Emile would never have considered important. If I craved an elegant tea set, or a striking lampshade, I'd tell him it was a gift from my parents and the matter was settled.

Emile loved to socialize and wanted to go out nightly. If we weren't visiting friends or relatives, we'd go to the movies or to see a play. Both our families and circle of friends took turns organizing dinner parties, and Emile never refused an invitation. But when the moment came for us to reciprocate, he couldn't face the amount of money required.

"It's absurd," he complained, "your relatives are filthy rich. I can't afford to throw parties the way they do. Better forget about it."

"I'll do everything myself," I answered. "I won't order anything from the caterer." I reminded him what a good cook I was and added that my mother would contribute until I convinced him. As years went by, I was always praised for my dinner parties.

Emile was very close to his two married sisters, Georgette and Hélène. One summer, our three families rented houses in Ras el Bar on the Nile's Delta. These spacious huts or *e'shas*, had several bedrooms and a large living room and kitchen. In those days, they were built yearly and dismantled at the end of the season. They were made of wood and mainly straw to allow the passage of air and create a rustic effect, unlike these recent brick and stones constructions. It used to be a lovely beach resort where the sweet Nile waters met the blue Mediterranean across a long tongue of land. We used to call this narrow stretch *languette*—or *al lessan*. It was a pier-promenade, and beyond its limits, up to the far horizon, one could see the dark grayish olive-green river mix with the bright indigo-blue sea. The warm orange reflections of the setting sun unfolded infinite combinations of colors. I loved the view from the promenade in mid-August the most, when the Nile flood turned the water into a reddish-brown opaque mixture. Then, the two bodies of water separated like a natural frontier between two continents.

There was a lot to do in Ras el Bar: swimming in sweet or salty waters, fishing, sailing on the *feluccas* over the quiet Nile, or for those who weren't sea-sick, taking boat rides over the Mediterranean. I loved swimming as a child. Unlike Emile's overweight sisters, I didn't care to be seen in a bathing suit with my extra pounds, and I didn't want to tan. I had a very delicate complexion—almost a redhead's. And I had promised my mother I'd never go out without my umbrella. Luckily, that summer, we had a *e'sha* all to ourselves while Georgette and Hélène shared another.

Our *e'shas* were at a walking distance. It was a real change from Cairo. The straw huts were square and slightly elevated with the bedrooms surrounding a central open-air courtyard. I loved to stay up at night, in the kitchen or on a divan, staring at the black shimmering sky. I'd wrap myself in a mosquito net like a spider caught in its own web. There was no electricity there. The gas and oil lamps generated wavering shadows in the half-disclosed huts, creating an unsubstantial, airy atmosphere. I imagined I was suspended in time, on a ship's front deck, floating in the middle of nowhere. My sisters-in-law were my only problem.

Georgette, Hélène and I got along fine, and took turns looking after the children. I met many friends from Cairo and Heliopolis in the cafés bordering the beaches. From there, we could watch the bathers and chat. Sometimes the children would bring back seashells or call us to see a medusa stranded on the shore surrounded by tiny crawling crabs. Ras el Bar was the crab lovers' paradise. These freshly caught crabs were sold daily by vendors along the cornice and around the *e'shas,* chanting "*Kaboria! Kaboria!*" Emile, who loved seafood a lot, was in heaven. He made new acquaintances easily and spent his time playing backgammon at the Casino Fouad that was built on stilts over the sea. Customers played dice, backgammon— commonly called *trictrac* or *tawla*—and all sorts of card games as they smoked their *narguileh*. We would meet him there for a refreshing iced grenadine or *khoushaf*—dried fruits soaked in rosewater syrup—while young boys swiftly hung fragrant jasmine necklaces on our chests. Some nights we would all go together to the Guerba, a long corridor of clear Nile water. We rented a *felucca* to get there. The *feluccas'* lights glided silently in succession like torches in a night procession. The Guerba glittered under the moonlight and the *feluccas'* lamps. I liked to swim then, be a part of the moon and stars. The bather's bodies glowed in the dark, became phosphorescent. I don't know why, nor what substance causes this wonder. No one spoke. Even the children's play was quieter.

During the day, when I was busy working around the *e'sha,* Emile visited his sisters, and they talked for hours about their relatives and personal affairs. They also liked to compare the cost of living in Ras el Bar with the one in Cairo. One afternoon, he came back home distraught, "I can't believe we've been throwing away money all these years." He was out of breath.

"What's the matter?" I tried to calm him down.

"How irresponsible I've been! You're so young. Can you believe that Georgette spends half what we spend on groceries?"

"How can that be?" I knew a storm was coming and I felt powerless.

"Go. Talk to her," he said. "I had delicious grapes over at her house at half the price we paid for them yesterday. And the vegetables and meat prices she pays are outrageously low. Something is definitely wrong."

I agreed entirely with everything he said. "What a fool I've been! From now on, I'll ask Georgette's advice and shop only where she does," I assured him. The kids were coming back full of sand and starving. It was time to welcome them and prepare something to eat. I set the table like an automaton. My mind worked at full speed. Our happiness was seriously threatened and I had to depend on all the resources of my imagination. I did not sleep all night. The next morning I visited Georgette and went shopping with her. Emile was pleased with my attitude.

From then on, when I'd serve him grapes, I'd crush some with my fingers. Strawberries and figs got the same treatment. Sometimes I'd run boiling water over the fruits for a second. I'd let the cheese sweat a little out in the sun. Emile would eat without a word. At times, he complained, "What's the matter with this cheese? Are you sure it's real kashkawan?"

"It is the exact same one your sisters bought this morning," I said. "True, we are saving more money—thanks to them."

When we returned to Cairo, Emile put up with this situation long enough to make me lose both hope and patience. Finally, after a few weeks, he said, "The hell with my sisters! I prefer our old lifestyle. You make your own decisions. You know better. I can't live the way they do."

See. This is happiness. This is what young people nowadays fail to understand.

MARIAM

It was becoming harder and harder to get the children to sleep. Mariam needed her rest, and the two little djinns' unbelievable energy increased at bedtime. And now, she thought, Laura and Kamil are going out more and more often. They went almost nightly to the open-air theaters that abounded in Heliopolis. When Kamil and Laura took the children along, they always invited Mariam. Although she only knew colloquial Arabic and could not even read the subtitles, shown in two or three languages, she enjoyed the succession of animated images.

But tonight she was home, and had to look after the children once more. She was not up to it, she sighed. She was no longer young and was exhausted from watching over boiling pots and frying pans for too many years. Her legs and feet, streaked with wrinkled veins, swelled at the end of the day, and the only way to ease the pain was to lie down and lift her feet up—that is, when the children would deign to close their eyes. Only then could she go to her room and rest.

The children seemed to believe that from the minute their parents left the house a new day dawned, full of promises. They did not care that Mariam's day was spent canning black and green olives brought directly from the *ezba*, a farm by the Delta. They did not realize the time it took to fill ten large jars with layers of olives, garlic cloves, slivered lemons and coarsely chopped celery, pour in olive oil, then seal them carefully, tightening the lids over squares of cotton cloth. They did not see her climb the tall ladder ten times to place the heavy jars in the sandara, the storage area above her bedroom.

Despite the tremendous effort required, stocking the jars was the part she really liked. Mariam was the only one in the household to ever go up to the sandara. She kept its large cast iron key in the pocket of her long flowered gown, as though it were the key to a safe. She wouldn't take a chance for the rest of the help to sneak in when she wasn't watching. Only Mariam knew exactly how many bottles of olive oil were left or if it was time to buy certain herbs or spices. Every afternoon or early evening, she would lie down, head wrapped in a bright colored scarf tied above her forehead. Reclined with hands crossed behind her head, in her favorite posture, she could almost see through the ceiling as though it were crystal. She'd stay awake for hours, staring in her mind's eye at the rice, grain and cereal sacks, the soap supply, recounting the pickled and canned vegetable jars, the variety of jams: figs, berries, sugar-glazed apricots and rose petals. That was her domain: verifying that the level of olive oil had not lowered in jars filled with goat cheese squares, watching for signs of mold in the jam. She regularly checked each corner of the sandara, making sure there were no traces of cockroaches, beetles or ants that might threaten the provisions. She would constantly realign rows of orange blossom water, rosewater, mulberry syrup, rose syrup, next to *dibs al rumman*, the dark pomegranate molasses and, of course, the transparent *arak* brought yearly from Lebanon. She beamed at the thought of the *makdouss*, tiny eggplants stuffed with walnuts and preserved in olive oil that were Kamil's favorites. She saw herself as the family's keeper. She remembered she needed to order some Samani dates from the *ezba*. That would be another long process: she would slice each date to remove the stone and stuff it with a blanched almond, a clove and a sliver of orange rind before simmering them in honey. The whole family craved these treats. "We have enough almonds," she thought, as she stroked her chin, "but I'll need to get some cloves." The tip of her chin bore a Coptic cross, similar to the one tattooed inside her right wrist, and she constantly rubbed it whenever preoccupied. She refused to think of tomorrow: today had been a very long day and she was eager to rest and review in her mind the latest addition to her treasure, the ten precious olive jars.

"I hope the children won't give me a hard time tonight," she mumbled as she wound her braids around her head, fastening them behind her ears with tortoise pins. Yet, some days it was impossible to keep them quiet. She didn't like to scare them, though. They were good kids. She loved them like her own. After all, she had assisted the Swiss midwife, Mrs. Spillman, when they were born. Laura was the first to admit that Mariam had raised them, repeating constantly to friends and relatives, "Bless her heart! What would we all become without Mariam?" Yes, she was more than a nanny, much more, and she knew her responsibilities. . . . At bedtime, she improvised, "I'll play with them a little first, comply with their demands. Then, I'll think of something," she muttered as she walked to the children's room. Charles and Simone had discovered a new game the day she agreed to loosen her long grayish braids. She had given in, hoping they would stop harassing her with their constant,

"Mariam, how long are your braids? Do they touch your knees? Show us! Show us!" Both decided immediately that she was their old pony, and took turns jumping on her chubby padded back, with braided reins in their hands, until she thought her poor back would break.

The children had seen *Prince Valiant* twice already and *Ivanhoe* for the fourth time this summer. Most of their recent games revolved around chivalry, and Charles' greatest dream was to become a knight—in fact, he had no doubt he was one.

"Hey, Simone," he said. "If you hold the reins halfway, you can whip the courser's flanks. I'll be the Black Knight, and you'll be Prince John."

"No. I'll be Lady Rowena, I'll wear my hair up."

"No way! I want a fair joust with a valiant knight, not with a weak weeping woman," said Charles. "Giddy up, ding dong, faster, faster! Faster!!"

"Aaaah! Akhkh! My back!" shrieked the unfortunate woman-centaur. "That's it, to bed! *Yallah!* To bed! Or else!"

They only paid attention to her when she said, stressing each syllable, "Aboushalom, the evil *afrit*, is coming for both of you tonight. He snatches sleepless children with his long fingernails and his thrice-forked tail. Stop moving, now. Close your eyes and go to sleep." She then turned the lights off as she slowly continued, "Aboushalom sees in the dark; he has five glowing eyes over his wide forehead."

The threats were not good enough. The children seemed more excited with the mystery of her imaginary Aboushalom. Charles disappeared under the cotton bedspread and kept jumping as if still riding underground, "Faster, faster!" while Simone meowed, "Help! Help me! I'm drowning!"

Silently, Mariam covered herself with a white sheet and put scotch tape on the light switch. She crawled stealthily several times around the beds repeating in a hoarse voice, "I am Aboushalom! Who is still awake?" No answer. No one moved. She kept circling until she heard them breathing evenly. It seemed to have worked. Things went more smoothly than she had expected, and she proclaimed victory in this last battle. I'll do it again, she thought, on her way to her retreat.

Mariam's room was right next to the kitchen, at the opposite end of the house from the other bedrooms. It was a very spacious room where she also folded laundry and ironed, adjacent to a corridor in which the brand new Philips refrigerator was standing. This made her location crucial to control the household movements. If anyone woke up with a craving at night, she was the first to know. She enjoyed living with the Chakers in that large apartment surrounded on each façade with several semi-circular verandahs. Mariam had spent most of her youth serving Laura's parents, the Boulos family and she recalled their beautiful villa situated behind the sepia-pink Maronite church, and close to the white-domed great Basilica of Heliopolis, copied after Istanbul's Hagia Sophia. When Laura married Kamil Chaker, in 1936, the faithful servant followed as part of her trousseau.

Mariam started out at the Bouloses doing a little of everything. Her mother had been in charge of the family laundry for many years. When her husband died, the laundress begged the Bouloses to employ the young girl. One summer, Mariam's mother took a long leave to visit relatives in a distant Rif village and never returned. She had a weak heart and died suddenly of a stroke. The orphaned girl gradually became indispensable around the house. She assisted the other maids in their many chores, making beds, folding laundry or ironing.

She also helped in the kitchen, when the Sudanese cooks were overwhelmed with work. The cooks were good to her and let her have a taste of the desserts and cookies they made daily. She remembered Abbas and Ahmed's black shiny faces. They had three parallel incisions on each cheek, forming the mark of the One Hundred and Eleven tribe, famous in Sudan for honesty and cleanliness. Sorting beans, chickpeas or lentils was her favorite occupation. The Sudanese would seat her by the large white marble table and show her how to separate the grain from stones and debris.

"See," Abbas would say, "these are good. They're whole. This one, with the tiny hole in it, you throw away."

"What if I miss some? Would we be eating wormy lentils?"

"Don't worry, Mariam," he said with a large smile showing his white teeth. "A tiny worm won't hurt you!"

Disgusted, she sorted carefully. With her index finger she placed the suspicious grain to the side, examining them closely, one by one, afraid they would slide back of their own will.

There, in the large basement kitchen, it was always teatime. The servants gathered around the table with tall glasses of dark boiled tea, whenever they had a break. Mariam always found their conversation intriguing. She thought of Ketty, the Greek governess, and Salwa, the Egyptian maid who read everyone's fortune in coffee dregs. "Tomorrow, we'll have guests," Salwa would say sententiously, looking at the bottom of the cup, "I see three lines converging into the center. In three days, Abbas, you will hear from your brother." With time, Mariam never made a decision before having coffee with Salwa.

She was happier now, though, despite the greater responsibility. She liked to be in charge. Mariam enjoyed the large window above her bed, unusual for a maid's room. Lucky that they were on the first floor, she always thought. The top branches of one of the fragrant henna trees almost reached her window, which she left open when the tree blossomed with tiny pale yellow flowers, its strong sweet scent, carried by the warm breeze, impregnating the whole room.

She massaged her hands with lotion, then crossed her fingers until she'd hear the knuckles crack, one by one. Reclined over pillows she contemplated the wall adjacent to her bed, entirely covered with saints' pictures. In the center, the Miraculous Virgin—arms uplifted, hands casting glowing rays—surrounded by Saint Barbara, patroness of good eyesight; Saint Agnes, whose long blond wavy hair grew instantaneously to cover her nudity and a youthful Saint Anthony of Padua, patron of lost objects and impossible quests, his brown tunic belted by a long cord. It was common then to dress babies for a whole year as Saint Anthony when they were very sick as a pledge of faith for their recovery. Black and white portraits of Charles and Simone as babies, alternated with snapshots taken at family reunions. There was one of Simone crying, holding the white kitten she had to abandon in Damascus, of Charles riding a camel at the Pyramids with the Sphinx in the background, and an enlarged picture of both children on a seesaw at the Heliopolis Sporting Club. She favored a year-old snapshot of herself with the whole family at the Sidi Bishr beach in Alexandria. Yes, these were great memories. She smiled, stroking her chin. She felt nostalgic about sunsets; she could almost feel the rhythm of the tide and the salty spray mixed with the henna fragrance pervading her room.

The children used to go to sleep faster in Alexandria, she thought, reminiscing. It must have been the sea breeze. She'd just begin telling a story, and they were already dreaming, the little angels, with their mouths open, tired from swimming and playing all day long in the wet sand by the turquoise waters. She enjoyed watching their games and helped them collect seashells and shiny rocks with intriguing shapes. They gathered a collection of enormous seashells from the Red Sea and Ras el Bar, which they insisted on taking along. She recalled the stories Simone and Charles liked most back then. As soon as they were sound asleep, she'd sit outside the summerhouse, resting her feet over pillows and she'd tell and retell herself the unfinished stories under the moonlight as she sipped strong dark tea in a tall glass. She'd bring the hollow seashells to her ear, attentive to their different calls: The Winged Conch's deep lament, the Spindle's murmur, the Murex's deafened whisper.

Some nights, she would hear a strange music and find herself surrounded by shimmering sea creatures led by a giant fish standing erect, covered with mica-like scales, his fins falling from around his large neck like a transparent cape. A sea horse with a starry crest, his incredibly long tail coiled around a musical score, accompanied him. These apparitions, flanked by a suite of glowing starfish jumping on the tip of their branches, illuminated the night and danced around her, telling her amazing stories.

At times, she'd rub the shells gently, one by one, but would only hear a distant hum, an undecipherable message. She then understood that the sea creatures needed to rest and tried to imagine an infinite variety of possible endings to their stories. She was getting short of new ideas, though, and looked once more at the images on the wall. Simone looked radiant on the seesaw with her white Shantung smocks. That day was the little girl's sixth birthday. The dress wasn't appropriate for the club, Mariam thought, remembering how she worried it could get stained or damaged by the swings.

It was in the Heliopolis Sporting Club that she refilled her provision bag of bedtime stories. Mariam watched the children at play while chatting with the other maids and nannies. There, gossip never stopped. True or false, the stories were always astounding, especially the innumerable tales her friend Samiha knew. Not only was Samiha's father a storyteller, but he had also trained his sons in the tradition. Samiha could not distinguish between the people she grew up with and the characters in her stories. She would often contradict herself, like that day when she insisted that her uncle was a silk and brocade merchant while everyone knew he worked in a falafel stand in Khan Khalili—Cairo's old section. Some maids did not believe her father had ever been a storyteller. To Mariam it did not matter at all; she could listen to Samiha forever.

The Chakers went regularly to the club on weekends. There, they would go their own way, oftentimes playing or watching games of squash, golf, cricket, tennis or bridge, and Mariam would follow the children in the areas reserved for them. There were several playgrounds and cafés overlooking the different sized pools, so thanks to Mariam, Khalil and Laura were able to socialize at leisure. During the summer, Mariam took Charles and Simone to the club's pool while Laura and her husband indulged in long afternoon siestas. The intense heat forced everyone to close the shutters while the sun toasted the city. Afternoon matinées at the indoor cinema Farouk, close to the Basilica, were also an option, and she'd often take them there.

At that theater they watched Arabic movies especially comedies starring the popular Ismail Yassine, the Egyptian counterpart to the French Fernandel or the Italian Toto. There were many comedians they would also watch at the Oasis open-air cinema. Mariam loved the Farouk's red velvet drapes, richly embroidered with gold stitching displaying two majestic iridescent peacocks ruffling their feather trains into multicolored-eyed fans. Both peacocks faced each other closely when the drapes were drawn, forming an imposing central shape surrounded with piercing eyes. Mariam nodded, rubbing her chin. Yes, she should check the upcoming movies. She needed to find ways to entertain the children before and after the long vacations they spent at the beach or in Lebanon. She loved staying at the Lebanese mountains in full-pension hotels where all she did was look after the children along with other nannies. There, they'd gather wild *zaatar*, a cross between oregano and thyme that she would dry, then mix with the local sumac and toasted sesame seeds to make *zaatar*. They would also pick young silky grape leaves they'd roll in tight packs and stuff in jars, making sure all the air was expelled: she usually brought back a few jars, enough to make stuffed grape leaves for a while. She smiled, imagining them lined up in the sandara. But now, in Heliopolis, she had to improvise daily to maintain Simone and Charles occupied. It would have been impossible to get them to take a nap with that heat. It was hard enough to put them to bed every night and invent a new engaging fable, she thought, sighing and stretching her arms above her head. She removed the tortoise pins and crossed her fingers under the nape of her neck.

She had already told them the story of the ghoul who looked like a Sphinx and blew hot fiery air, destroying everything he encountered. His name was Abul Hol. Whenever he was not obeyed, he took multiple shapes, flattening entire cities with the palms of his hands. Yes, she nodded at the pictures on the wall, and they are getting tired of it.

They still liked the story of the man whose left leg swelled and swelled until he couldn't walk. He had to stop his long journey and abandon the caravan he traveled with. He settled in the first small oasis they encountered in the middle of the desert. His camel and a goat were his only company. He had some fresh water his companions gave him in case the water was polluted. The caravan men thought the water had to be contaminated; otherwise, the oasis wouldn't be abandoned. They wondered if an evil *afrit* had cast a spell on it—or if it had actually become some djinns' dwelling. It was well known that djinns and *afrits* loved to settle by any source of water. This increased their powers.

Charles was always perplexed at this point of the story and wanted to know more about these fleeting spirits called djinns and their evil counterparts, the *afrits*. He was also concerned with the man's survival in case the water was poisoned. Mariam had to remind him that the man had to deal with more pressing problems than the water. After resting a day or two, he felt increasing tension and a throbbing pain inside his swelling leg. He took the sharp knife he used to cut date clusters, sharpened it on a wet stone, and carefully opened a long deep slit along his shin. He found a baby girl. He tore his white cotton shirt in two. In one half he wrapped the newborn child, and the other half he cut in long strips to bandage his bleeding, gaping wound. The baby grew, thanks to the goat's milk, and became a young girl as beautiful as the moon on its fourteenth day. The man's wound healed but left him limping heavily, and he could not climb the palm trees anymore. He relied on the young girl to cut leaves and dates from the taller trees. One day he died of a sudden fever and left the girl unprotected.

The children loved the part where the caravan of a rich silk merchant's son approached, bringing back merchandise from Damascus. When the young man saw the naked adolescent girl, a twin to the full moon, hiding in the tallest palm tree, he decided to take her as his bride. He clothed her in his most precious embroidered silks from tip to toe and took her back to his hometown. There, he sent her to the *hammam* where she was bathed and perfumed, before he presented her to his parents as a lost princess. This story always captivated the children, especially Simone, who wanted more and more details about the girl's embroidered muslin shirt, her long gathered pants and veils, and about what happened in the *hammam*.

But tomorrow, what should she tell them? Mariam worried, yawning and readjusting the pillow under her feet. She had to think of something ahead of time. Tomorrow, Zeinab the laundress was coming, and Mariam would have to help hang the laundry on unending ropes all over the terrace. Then Laura and Mariam would fold batches and batches of dry stiff clothes and linen. It was windy up there, on the terrace. Mariam often felt the clothespins stick to her fingers, lifting her up, as if they had grown wings. She would fight the pull, fastening the clothespins with all the strength left in her raised hands. Last week, the wind had draped the cold, damp sheets around her, shrouding her body and face. She felt ready to take off as if on a magic carpet over the roofs, terraces, streets, tramways and gardens of Heliopolis.

She wondered if Zeinab had anything to do with all of this. She pictured Zeinab in the little room in the corner of the terrace, standing beside two boiling cauldrons, her reddened face suffused with sweat, receding, seemingly distant through the fuming steam. She stood there for hours, stirring and wringing the foamy clothes with long wooden tongs. At times, she added a handful of white, yellow or blue powder, as if mixing herbs and roots in a secret brew.

On laundry days, Mariam dreaded going up and down the stairs all day long. She carried the meal trays, not to mention the laundry baskets, and refilled the Primus kerosene burners. "No," she muttered to herself, shaking her head, "I'll have no break, not a minute to myself." I'd better be prepared for bedtime, she thought. She would invoke Aboushalom only in case of emergencies. Better to have a good story for tomorrow. Had she told them recently the story of the rotten lentils and the two sisters? She was not sure anymore . . . maybe the lentils weren't rotten at all. No, she thought, there were worms in the lentil sack. She remembered having told them this story a long time ago. They must have forgotten it by now.

Mariam stared at the ceiling, conjuring scenes and visions, and recalled: There were two orphan sisters who were very, very poor. They lived in a small house, the only possession their parents had left them. The two sisters grew a small vegetable garden and wove straw baskets they sold in the village's souk. One year, it barely rained. Crackled dry earth replaced what once had been a green, luscious food supply. The village well was almost dry, and water was cautiously rationed.

The two sisters survived, thanks to their reserve of fava beans, rice, corn, lentils and chickpeas, all stored in big rugged sackcloth. One day, the younger sister said, "I found worms in the lentils. I think we should throw them away."

"No," said the older sister, "a day will come when we would need them. We will sort them out and eat the good ones."

"But it will be very difficult, and we will end up eating some with worms inside. Let's throw them away," argued the younger. And they went on and on, and the younger sister would bring the subject up every day until her older sister said, "Have it your way, but some day you will be sorry." And the younger one threw out the lentils without delay.

The drought intensified. Now the two sisters had barely enough water to drink and cook the dry cereals. Food was getting scarcer, and the girls reached the point when they traded their baskets for whatever leftovers they could get. The older sister kept repeating every single minute, "If you hadn't thrown the lentils away we wouldn't be working for nothing. We could have lasted a few more weeks with these lentils." On their way to the village, the oldest would say, "If you hadn't thrown the lentils away we wouldn't have to live like beggars." At night, when their stomachs were growling with hunger pangs, in a faint, sleepy voice the oldest would mumble, "If you hadn't thrown the lentils away . . ." In a moment of desperation, the younger sister took a knife and shut her sister up. Horrified by her terrible deed, she buried her older sister where the vegetable garden had grown.

A few months later, it rained again and life returned to its normal course. The younger sister told whoever asked about her sister, "She preferred to leave with some other families in search of a better place to live." Years went by, and the younger sister married an honest man, Omar, the only son of the village's respected *mokhtar*. He made her very happy and gave her two strong and beautiful sons who helped her take care of their now-splendid vegetable garden. Omar had planted fruit trees year after year all around it, and now, some of the fruit was gradually ripening.

One mulberry tree in particular, had beautiful thick shiny dark green leaves. Its branches came right through the younger sister's kitchen window, heavy with berries for the first time. I'll fill a large bowl for the family, she thought, and began picking the dark purple fruit. She tasted the pulpous berries gluttonously, mindless of staining her hands, mouth and dress, when a familiar voice coming from the tree said, "If you hadn't thrown the lentils away. . ." And her children saw her running quickly in one single direction with blood on her hands and dress. No one ever understood what had happened. She never came back.

They would like this one, Mariam thought. At least she was all set for tomorrow night. She'd try to avoid Aboushalom. No. Only in case of necessity. She slid another pillow under her legs and tried to make herself as comfortable as possible. Yawning deeply, she wondered what day it was. Friday? The day after tomorrow was Sunday. They'll spend part of the day at the club. There, she thought, I'll ask Samiha to retell me the story about the prince who dared enter the translucent alabaster house on an inaccessible cliff guarded by a white-winged horse. This one was Mariam's favorite. She could not remember the prince's name; was it Shams or Badr? Whose left eye was snatched by the hawk with the golden beak for opening the house's seven forbidden doors? Mariam asked herself. The first door led to a garden filled with mounds of gems, glowing like a thousand suns: pearls, corals, emeralds, topazes, amethysts, turquoises, diamonds and sapphires, some the size of a dove's egg.

What did the second door lead to? Mariam tried to remember, as she rubbed her raised legs, flattening her protruding veins with her fingertips. The second door led to a garden in which the blossoming trees were heavy with all sorts of birds, singing the most harmonious melodies, echoed by the murmur of fountains, brooks and rivulets. She could not remember what marvels were hidden behind the other doors. But Samiha would surely know. The children will love this one, Mariam sighed, eyes half-closed. She was sleepy now. . . .

She sensed the presence of the sea creatures dancing rhythmically about the room. In a half-dream she felt Charles and Simone by her side, attracted by the music that was becoming louder and louder. As the sea creatures circled around them faster and faster, she felt the sea breeze and her wet feet. She held the children tighter and could no longer distinguish the sea creatures whirling in an infernal round, pulling them into the deepest darkness. Before she closed her eyes she saw the creatures' faces merge into one face with five glowing eyes, the face of Aboushalom.

12 RUSHDY STREET

I had often dreamt of going back to Egypt, to the house where I grew up, in Heliopolis, and of taking a long trip along the Nile to Upper Egypt. The vivid image of a *felucca* gliding over dark mirroring waters was always present in my mind, a flowing backdrop to the final act Amin and I might once have played. But that was a long time ago—before Paris, before Pierre— Parisian life, an escape at first, began to weigh on me, tying me with invisible strings.

After more than twenty years in Paris, I was finally able to break away from the routine, my job at the Cité Universitaire, and above all from my tenants whose vacations finally coincided with mine for the first time in ages. Ever since Pierre had died from a heart attack, seven years ago, I had been renting rooms so I wouldn't come back to an empty house at the end of the day, but I could not have found a better way to lose my freedom. I felt more responsible for the young girls who lived with me than I would have if they had been my own children.

I landed at the Heliopolis' airport and went straight to the Palace Hotel. As soon as the car stopped at the Palace's arched door, tall clerks gathered around the taxi in their elegant *gallabiyas* and fought ceremoniously over my few pieces of luggage, inviting me with gestures to follow them. I felt I was the lead in an old black-and-white movie that could have taken place in Cairo or in New Delhi—anywhere the British had left their imprint. The discreet wallpaper, the dark paneling and even the portly leather furniture resting on Persian carpets reflected their presence.

Throughout the vast, crowded lobby the waiters revolved from one end to another, their long *gallabiyas* fastened with thick embroidered belts the same color as the *tarabeesh* covering their heads, swerved as in a folkloric ballet, balancing trays filled with plates covered with shining silver lids. I followed a porter up the coral-red carpeted stairs to my room and ordered a light snack that I took in the semi-circular balcony overlooking a patio framed with purple bougainvilleas. Later, I took a short nap, from which I suddenly awoke, perplexed by a dream in which all the streets' names in Heliopolis were French.

I decided to take the tramway to rediscover the city, since I had been familiar with the tram and bus routes when I was a child. I had no specific destination in mind. The frequent stops that shook the compartments allowed me to study everything around me and to recall the stations' names. As we passed the Palace Theatre, then the Normandy Theatre, I imagined familiar silhouettes pressing themselves in line for the tram. I glanced at the half-empty terrace of the Palmyra café, famous for its Viennese coffee—Amin's favorite.

So many people had fled Egypt and Nasser's regime during the past years that there was hardly anyone left I might have known. I felt this suburb of Cairo had been invaded by alien faces, overcrowding the streets that suddenly seemed, foreign, exotic. I recognized Midan Ismailia, then Midan Saphir where I stepped out from my compartment. The streets and sidewalks of Heliopolis appeared so much dustier as if no one had swept or washed them for decades. Even the central avenues were neglected. The lawn and trees were parched, begging to be watered. I had forgotten it never rained in Heliopolis.

Midan Saphir must have drastically changed, or my memory of the place had been completely erased. I walked Rushdy Street nervously, my heart pounding, afraid my old house wouldn't be there anymore. The house—number twelve—stood as always, at an angle to Rushdy Street. I faced the three-story house that had haunted me all my life. The more I looked at it, the more familiar the house became, in the same way that we rediscover the youthful features of an old friend after a long absence, through a smile or an expression. The house had the imposing grace of certain old people who have aged well. The first floor's main verandah led to the garden through wide, white marble stairs, but the elegant mental image I had of this stairway was marred by a wooden fence around the verandah.

A few steps ahead, just beyond the wrought-iron front gate, two henna trees still stood behind the tall stone pillars, exactly as I remembered them, perhaps a little shorter. When we were out at night, my old cat, Soumass always awaited us like a Sphinx on top of one of those pillars. I imagined Soumass in broad daylight, stern, phlegmatic, staring at me from both sides with the majesty of the bronze lions flanking the Kasr el Nil Bridge in downtown Cairo. I began to recognize the house as my own, although the façade had not been painted for ages, and the plaster was falling off in places like heavy makeup drying on a wrinkled face.

I passed the fragrant henna trees and pushed open the heavy double-paned glass and wrought iron door that led to the stairwell. The first thing I noticed was the janitor's room at the bottom of the staircase, facing the entrance. I'd always wondered how our janitor could stand living in this window-less, low-ceilinged room that forced him to bend every time he entered through the square wooden door. I pictured him always out at night, sitting on a pillow on the floor by the main door, in the lotus position, delaying the moment he'd have to shut himself inside the room as if he were entombed in the center of a pyramid.

I rang the doorbell. When no one answered, I tried the side door and waited a while, but behind the closed doors there was silence. Three sisters had lived here, years ago. The youngest, Sherine, and I had been very good friends.

I decided to go to the second floor, where my family and I used to live. When my father bought this house, it was designed for a single family with several servants and a number of guestrooms. My father preferred to divide the house into three individual apartments. He had the staircase rebuilt, added a few bathrooms and expanded the kitchens on each floor. We lived on the second floor and rented the first and third floors. Everyone shared the terrace for laundry and storage.

At my first ring, a young girl of about eighteen, in her school uniform, opened the door. I recognized on her pocket the intertwined initials "MD" of the high school I had attended: Mère de Dieu. I introduced myself: "My family owned this house a long time ago. I lived in this apartment until my marriage and have been living in Paris since then."

"Paris? Come in," she said. "My parents will be back soon."

I refused her invitation and asked about the first floor neighbors, not at all surprised to learn that the three girls were married and that the oldest still lived here with her grandchildren—which explained the intrusive wooden fence.

"They are in the country at the moment," the girl said.

"And who lives on the third floor?"

"We do," she replied. "When my father bought this house seven years ago, he converted the second and third floors into a duplex. We added an interior staircase."

"Can I go up to the terrace? I'd like to take a look at the neighborhood. Or is someone living there?"

"No," she said. "The door is open."

Left alone, I paused and thought of the evenings when Amin and I watched the city lights from the terrace. The Riviera Theater's neon sign glittered as if pinned over one of the brilliant stars. I remembered how I climbed these stairs, two or three at a time, every single day. As I climbed now the white-veined marble stairs, the darkness increased as I went up; the steps became narrower, the walls seeming to close in on me. I didn't remember the terrace being so far up. I kept climbing, increasingly oppressed. But now, it was more arduous with each step, and I could almost feel the walls rubbing against my right arm and shoulder. Then, somehow, the concrete receded, seemed insubstantial. I tried to move faster. I saw faces smiling, pulling me through the misty, whitewashed walls, transporting me to a scene from my youth: *the milkman chases me on his bike one Sunday morning. I am only thirteen and on my way to an early mass. I start running fast, breathless, my uncomfortable first high heels slowing me down. I stumble like a duck with glued wings. I run faster, horrified at the sight of the milkman's long gown pulled up, uncovering a huge erection. I finally reach the door of a friend's house.*

I longed for the fresh air beyond the terrace's door. I had to escape, avoid the uninvited, unwanted faces, deceiving me with their smiles and whispers, slowing me down. The staircase narrowed and twisted into a spiral. I could not see its end in the dark. It was like rushing to the top of a lighthouse. I made a final effort. I could see the door now. I was a few steps away from breathing freely again. I tried to open the door with all my strength, but it was locked. I had to get out, out of the staircase, the house, the darkness. I ran down the stairs faster than I'd ever run before, already imagining myself outside, running down the middle of the street and not looking back. But there was no way out at the bottom of the stairwell, only a gaping opening beneath a steep, narrow step, like the bottomless entrance to an underground.

I rushed to the second floor frantically and pushed the doorbell, afraid that no one would answer. The girl appeared and looked at me with surprise and concern.

"Don't you feel well?"

I could not utter a word. I was certain that she could hear my heartbeat, or see my heart leaping in my chest. I made a tremendous effort to stay calm, anchoring my legs to the ground to stop them from shaking.

"Come in," she said. "I'll bring you a cup of coffee. Please sit down."

I sat obediently in the corner of the white damask sofa. She left for a minute, then came back with a glass of lemonade.

"How do you prefer your coffee?" she asked with a smile.

"*Mazbout*," I said.

The room was permeated by a soothing atmosphere, comparable to the one an exhausted desert traveler experiences when he finally rests in the shade of tall palms in a long-sought oasis. As she left, I noticed the black and white checkered marble floor: small black diamonds surrounded with large white squares, the same pattern I'd kept in my mind all this time. I contemplated the room's four pillars and ornate ceiling. The furniture and the Persian rugs were unfamiliar, as was the spiraling staircase, with its bronze railings. The staircase blocked the area where our bedrooms had once been. I felt an urge to go to my parent's bedroom, lie on their king size bed, and see once more the pink satin bedspread and the lace curtains with frolicking cupids. I had always lain in my parents' bed when I was sick, imagining myself a part of the curtains' pastoral scenes.

The lemonade was cool and refreshing. I felt much better and even managed to smile at the young girl as she reentered the room carrying a copper coffee tray.

"Do you live alone in Paris?" she said, as she handed me the coffee cup.

"Yes, in a way. My husband died a few years ago and we never had children. But I rent rooms to students. I work at the Cité Universitaire."

"My boyfriend studies in Paris," she said. "He's an architect. I wanted to study literature at the Sorbonne, but my parents won't let me because Nadim is there."

Nadim. Amin. Paris. It all came back as if it were happening again. Amin and I. Our destiny had also been connected to Paris. I had always had an impossible dream—to study art at the Beaux-Arts in Paris—but in those days it was unthinkable for a girl to travel or live alone abroad. Then Amin came along and I forgot all about Paris for years, until he spent a long summer there, training as a civil engineer in Ponts et Chaussées, after which he decided to end our relationship. "It won't work," he said, "but it's not because I don't love you anymore." I never learned his reasons and never saw him again. I worked at an attorney's office where I met Pierre. We ended up living in Paris. Years later, I heard that Amin was in Paris married to a French girl.

And now, this girl, wanting to go to Paris. Like me at her age. I offered to send her information about student life in the Cité and to save her a room in my house in case she decided to come. Maybe her parents would feel more comfortable knowing someone would guide her over there. She would really like the other girls, I thought.

She could not stop asking me about Paris, the plays, the museums, everything. "I can't wait to be there," she sighed.

"If it were not for Nadim, my parents would let me go. They are worried about what people would say."

"I will still be at the Palace a few more days. I would gladly talk to your parents any time," I assured her. "Although this Saturday I'm going to Upper Egypt from Cairo. By boat."

"Can you believe I have never been to Luxor and Aswan!" she exclaimed, opening her eyes in wonder.

"Yes. I can," I nodded as I grabbed my purse and stood.

"Could you accompany me down the stairs?" I asked. "You wouldn't mind, would you?"

"Not at all."

"High blood pressure," I felt obliged to explain. "It runs in my family."

She walked me out as if I were an old friend or a relative.

"I am so glad to have met you," she repeated. "Paris . . . I can't believe it will happen." I smiled at her enthusiasm.

"I'll call you at the Palace. You don't mind? There's so much I'd like to know!" Her words were enveloping me like the softly perfumed breeze flowing through the door. She talked incessantly as she led me to the sweet-scented henna trees.

* * *

The trip to Luxor and Aswan appeared to me in retrospect as a succession of extended sunsets, or a series of paintings in which the horizon is only broken at times by silhouettes of *fellahin*, going about their chores, palm trees or temple pillars. Back in Paris, I kept within me a feeling of weightlessness, as if the openness of Egypt's forever-blue sky had filled my veins. I gradually sank into my daily routine. To each young face, I would juxtapose the Egyptian girl's face, as if I expected to see her everywhere. I made all the necessary arrangements for her to stay with me and began compiling a file with all the information that I thought might interest her and, most of all, convince her parents to let her come. I wanted to give her the best welcome.

Somehow my life had a new purpose: the happiness of this young Egyptian girl whom I had only seen twice. I remembered her last, drinking tea on the Palace's patio, admiring the bougainvillea, and talking, talking. I kept a list of all her questions and concerns. I explored the registration offices, campus life, the students' meals and activities, as if I were about to become part of it all. I enjoyed spending my lunch hour in the cafeterias, mimicking the students' attitudes, and smiling to myself for no reason. The eternal drizzle of Paris, its grayness—to which I had never grown accustomed—now ceased to affect me.

During that period, I had recurrent dreams about my spell in the staircase, but I tried to avoid thinking about them. I'd wake up anguished, imagining myself struggling against different sized doors with strangely shaped locks. It took a while before I could convince myself it was only a dream. I became more claustrophobic than I'd ever been and I—who had always hated elevators—chose to take the elevator instead of the stairs whenever possible.

Still, there was no way that I could completely avoid stairs, not in Paris at any rate. I had to take the metro daily and many buildings had no elevators. Most of the time I was able to control my fear, but not always. One day in the metro's corridor, I was surrounded by people hurrying home with their usual blank expressions. I suddenly felt separated from the crowd, who didn't notice that the walls were shaking, sliding towards the middle of the corridor as if both sides were about to meet. I ran forward in a frenzy, pushing and elbowing people. I wanted to shout, yet was unable to emit a single sound. Only one image filled my mind: I saw myself emerging from the darkness toward the sweet-scented henna trees.

The henna trees. The girl. I realized that my feelings of entrapment in the staircase that day in Rushdy Street had created in me a constant tension that was only alleviated by the girl's image. I was anxious to see her again. I pictured her making plans, excited, yet I couldn't help worrying. My dreams began to take another shape: I found myself circling amidst gigantic temple pillars, unable to find a way out, whirling and spinning like a dervish at the point of exhaustion. Just before I'd collapse, she'd take me by the hand and gently lead me towards the open.

One evening, as I was coming home, tired, I mechanically took my mail, and noticed an Egyptian stamp on one of the envelopes. I hurried to my apartment, took off my gloves, shoes, and coat. I lay comfortably on my bed as I opened the letter.

I slowed down at ". . . thank you for caring so much. You do not need to send me more details. I am not coming to Paris. Nadim has written to me saying that he is marrying his professor's daughter. . . ." The beginning and the end of the letter seemed blurry—only these sentences appeared clearly, as if they were three-dimensional. They seemed to jump out from the page, and then to recede into a thick fog just as the visions of my past had in the staircase. I felt trapped within the letter, within the walls, within my memories. . . .

II

GREEN FIGS AND CHERRIES

"Have you slept well?" an acrid voice shrills, tearing the intricate nets and webs unfolding around me. Eyes closed, I try to cling to the visions in my dream. I see myself dancing barefoot on a veined marble floor, revolving rhythmically among swinging hips. Strong arms seize me by the shoulders, lift me gently and slip a pillow behind my back. "Here, I'm going to take care of you," the nurse says. "It won't take long. Be patient; it may sting a little because of the antiseptic."

An uncomfortable sensation shakes me as she slides a white washbasin beneath me, the cold enamel touching my skin like an unwanted lover. "Bend your knees. Don't worry, it won't hurt. There, I'll leave the disinfectant bottle in the bathroom. Don't forget to mix its content with warm water every time you wash. Now, I want you to take a few steps around the room. Hang on to me. That's good." In the semi-darkness, my half-open eyes shift from the woman's angular face to the unfamiliar furniture and rug of the recovery room. I feel awkward, weak, helpless.

"I'll be back soon with your lunch," she says as she slowly opens the wooden shutters that creak feebly, resisting a little. Broken rainbows tremble, grow wider and wider, merge in a full sheet of golden light over my bed; reveal the geometric red and blue-gray designs of the Oriental rug. My family recommended Dr. Nasra's clinic—one of the best, according to my cousins who occupied that very same room upon giving birth. I remember visiting them with my mother. It was always such a happy occasion, an opportunity to meet other relatives. Everybody agreed that a private clinic provided much more warmth than a hospital's barrenness. The care was good and food excellent. It was supposed to feel like home.

The nurse nests me on double pillows, shows me how to use the remote control to reach a comfortable position. I hate electric or mechanical devices. I remember the hotel Claridge in Paris, our honeymoon, Selim setting the vibrating mattress full speed. It made me think of roller coasters, and all those rides I hated because of the intense pull. Always afraid of heights, a powerful elation would overcome me. I'd feel like throwing myself down; taking leave of my estranged body. I think I experienced something similar, though mixed with pleasure, when I first met Selim. It seems so long ago. It was at Leila's birthday party. I couldn't stay away from him. I wore my yellow sundress, the same color as the fluffy mimosas blooming in the avenues. Everyone said it suited my dark tan. Nada told me it put gold in my eyes. Restless, I smoked cigarette after cigarette waiting for Selim to ask me for another dance. When he came up to me, I heard myself say, as though reciting someone else's line, "Let me finish this one." We were the last to leave that night.

In the car he said, "Let's get married. I'll take care of everything. We could be in Paris next week for our honeymoon. We'll walk in the Bois de Boulogne before it gets too cold and stay at the Claridge. It's on the Champs Elysées, a few steps from that popular pub where most of our friends meet. Many are getting ready to go back to the Cité Universitaire for the fall semester."

We decided to skip the formalities, all the tedious invitations and ceremonies. Our parents would never forgive us, of course, but we figured we'd make better use of that money. We were so excited about seeing the latest plays and shows! I had never been to Paris. I could only think of his eyes. . . . It seemed too good to be true.

My aunts used to say, "Marriage is like a wrapped gift. No matter how well you think you know the man you're going to marry, you'll only know him the day you're married." So, I thought, what difference would it make if we waited? Days, weeks, months wouldn't change the way we felt about each other. It was the real thing. We both knew it.

As I watch the spring sun flood the room furnished to look like home with its dark, old furniture, I recall my visits, as a child, to my grandmother's relatives. Old maids and widows, whose homes remained unchanged through generations. Old-fashioned macramé protecting sofas' arms and headrests. Even the dust seemed untouched by time. That stillness preserved their youth, allowed their collapsing bodies to go on living among the shapes, smells and ways of the time when they and everyone around them were young. We used to visit them on holidays, especially during long summer evenings. I remember the dim light. Maybe they were saving electricity or feared the sun's rays would disclose dust and wrinkles. Smiling old ladies serving mulberry or rose petal syrup and small *maamoul* pastries on silver trays covered with handmade lace. With shaky hands, they passed their offerings, over and over again, insisting we sample their homemade treats.

I look at the bedside table's oval tapestry, surprised to find the phone still there. I had hurtled it onto the floor hours ago when the nurse refused to call the doctor. She sounded like a dummy reciting a lesson, "We have to wait; we're not supposed to call him until the dilation is sufficient," and to my mother, "Please, try to reason with your daughter—doctor's orders. There's nothing he can do at this point." And my pain, no one seemed to care about it. Mother held my hand to comfort me. "These breathing exercises don't work!" I begged, "I've changed my mind. I want a painless delivery. Call the doctor. Tell him to give me an epidural. It wasn't supposed to last so long." I grabbed my mother's chubby arm and dug my nails into her soft flesh.

Selim's mother would have liked this fashionable clinic. She was a nouveau riche, after all. "You could have married much later," she often told him. "A man of any age can marry an eighteen-year-old girl, a pretty one too—with a dowry. Look at yourself, so good looking, you'll still break women's hearts in your late forties." I was so much in love I could not see how insulting her comments were. I felt Selim deserved a better bride. I brought no cash into his family. My father's business was unpredictable. A self-made businessman, he made enough money to maintain a comfortable lifestyle, but not enough to offer a dowry—still an important issue in most families. I worried about losing Selim, because of his good looks, his perfect figure, his charisma. He told me how ecstatic his sisters were every time he wore a new shirt or sweater, "Wow! Shouldn't Selim always wear blue-green shades? It brings out so many facets in his eyes!" His eyes, so deep and striking I could never get enough of them! I always felt inferior, seeking ways to compensate with care and special attentions. But nothing was ever good enough for him, or for his mother. Then, I began to wonder, "Why did he blindly accept his mother's points of view?" When I understood that he could have kept to himself her constant, hurtful criticisms, it was too late: my waist was getting larger.

And where is my baby now? This room will remain as it is. No visits, chocolates, flowers. No opening of the baby's layette. Friends and relatives won't ask to see the baby. Nobody will say, "He looks exactly like his dad," or "He has his mother's eyes." There won't be fights over whose smile he has. No one will see my satin nightgown encrusted with Calais lace.

Where is Mother? Is she angry with me? Did I hurt her arm last night? Outside the window, I hear vendors praising green figs and cherries. I imagine them pushing carts over the hilly streets, wiping their moist necks and foreheads, "Bikfaya's peaches. Sample my delicious peaches!" Bikfaya's peaches' white perfumed flesh under pink and white velvety skin, I used to peel for Selim. I'd never be good enough for him. Could I ever please him? He kept saying, "Ask my mother how to do *kebbe*. Ask my sister Amy. She's a terrific cordon-bleu."

We had only been married a couple of months, and I wished I could forget it all like a bad dream. I'd wake up and return an unwrapped gift. With Selim gone for the weekend, I decided to spend some time with my parents. I found my mother struggling with different skeins of yarn. She'd move closer to the window, examining closely samples she stretched between her fingers. "I can't distinguish the shades anymore, even in broad daylight," she complained. So, I helped her disentangle the threads of the pastel balls dangling over the back of the divan. Unraveling, they rolled in all directions over the bright-colored Tabriz rug. We sipped our Turkish coffee quietly. We liked to drink it boiling hot—almost a ritual. I always turned the cup upside down to interpret the running coffee grounds' configurations. She scolded me, "Still a child! You already know your luck."

I told her about my sleepless nights, the endless reproaches. I tried to explain the tightness in my chest, my need to go away. She worried, "Things will get better. You must be patient. You're about to become a mother! Don't you know children strengthen ties between man and wife?"

"I can't take it anymore. I've tried. It's useless," I said. She shook her head angrily, "You know how divorced women are looked upon? Is this what you want for your child? Have you forgotten you'll have to give him up to his father at age nine? How will you feel then?" I imagined my child having to suddenly adjust to his father's family, maybe to a stepmother.

I had no choice, except to go back to Selim and make the best of the situation. I'd give a stable, if not a happy home to my child. I spent the last months of my pregnancy avoiding everybody. I read and reread maternity books. I was living in a separate world in which Selim and his family were perpetually intruding.

My breasts hurt so much. The doctor gave me pills to stop the milk flow, to take every five or six hours. "Your breasts will swell and be tender for a couple of days," he said. The nurse applied pads to absorb the dripping. I remember watching my sister nursing—the baby's mouth cupping her turgescent nipple, letting no drops escape. Sometimes, his tiny hand strongly gripped her finger, perhaps seeking her strength while sucking.

"Here's your lunch. Eat while it's hot. Vegetable soup and chicken." I dare not ask what my baby is eating. The nurses must follow strict instructions. Anyway, I know newborn babies aren't fed during the first hours.

"Don't worry, the baby will be fine," my mother said. "I ruined my figure nursing the four of you for eleven months. Now, women only nurse a couple of months. This isn't nursing; one may as well start bottle-feeding the baby. Besides, take your cousin Tina for example; she had no milk and look at her two handsome and healthy boys."

We decided I wouldn't see the baby. I'd have to be strong. If I were leaving, I should detach myself from the very beginning and let my husband worry about his child. My father kept repeating as though to convince himself, "You'll see, it's better this way. A mother is always a mother. When the child grows up he will get closer to you. You'll see."

The sun is completely gone now, leaving behind a fading light. I adjust the bed to a horizontal position and close my eyes. How could I agree not to feed my baby? Not ever see him, hold him? What if I lost my visiting rights later on? I just can't imagine him in my mother-in-law's arms.

I remember my last month of pregnancy at my parents' home, the daily discussions, my determination to begin a new life.

"I'm not going back. It's over."

"You know you'll be paying a great price for your freedom," my mother said.

"I can't go back."

"Then you shouldn't even see the baby. It will be better in the long run. You'll see. Time heals everything. His widowed grandmother will raise him since Selim moved in with her. And even if he remarried, she's bound to live with him because he is the oldest."

"Absolutely," my father added. "You will be saving yourself and the child so much pain and trouble. If you'd raised him for nine years, believe me, not too many men would be interested in you. Do you want to live alone the rest of your life?"

Marry. I'll never marry again. All I want is my baby, now. I ring the bell insistently until the nurse comes in running.

"Anything wrong? It's not time for your pills yet."

"I don't need these pills anymore. I want to nurse my baby."

"But, the doctor . . ."

At this moment, my mother enters the room.

"Have you seen the baby, Mother? Is it a boy or a girl?"

"A beautiful little boy," she says, wiping her tears.

"I want to see him. Bring him to me," I demand. "Bring him to me!"

The two women look at each other and leave the room. I know I'm doing the right thing. No one will care for my baby boy like me, his mother. I'll call him Samir and he will have the best life until he is old enough to understand. He will always remember me. I recline against the pillows, heart beating. Why is it taking so long?

Finally, he is in my arms, so tiny, so perfect. I hold him tight, lamenting he has lost the comfort of my womb. "Can I nurse him now?" Silently, the nurse's eyes interrogate my mother who says firmly: "You can go. I'll take care of everything." Helping me unfasten my bra, she kisses me while the baby's tiny mouth moves frenetically from right to left, trying to secure the swollen nipple. Is it too large for him? He cries, helpless. . . . I press him against my breast until he starts sucking with unsuspected strength. The room is almost dark. Seated by the edge of the bed, Mother places her hand on my legs, nodding her head rhythmically, smiling and crying silently. No one will ever separate me from Samir. I had chosen Selim, maybe hastily, but I know we can work it out. I will return to him. Everything will be fine. I know it. My baby sleeps now, mouth open, as I listen to his warm, regular breath.

DISTANCES

Up and down the Lebanese mountain village's most frequented promenade, summer vacationers linger, an invigorating breeze filtering through thick green layers of pine needles. A caravan of cars patiently wends its way upward, tired faces peering from windows, leaving behind deserted homes and offices, the stifling August air. They have driven around the mountain through curves and loops for half an hour, an hour, sometimes longer, longing for dry, cool sheets smelling of lavender and wildflowers.

The girl and the boy walk side by side along the crowded, winding road, part of the ebb and flow of passersby who have just awakened from their afternoon siesta. Like all mountain dwellers, they have forgotten what it was like to wake up in Beirut and desperately try to wipe off the persistent dampness of sticky sheets under a cold shower. In the mountains for a couple of months, they have forgotten how boring they had thought it was to be there, despite their parents' eternal praise of the healthy, vivifying air and the peaceful, relaxing greenness. They have forgotten many things, how often they had pleaded each year to stay home and swim, water-ski or go to the movies and beach parties. And now they are unable to face the fact that their vacation is coming to an end.

For generations, the boy's parents have owned a house in Reyfoun—an old stone summer house with a red-tiled roof and an interior patio with a mosaic fountain in its midst—where he has spent his summers for as long as he can remember. The girl's family has been coming to the Al Masyaf Hotel for three years, finding the meals delicious—the chef knows what he is doing, her parents often repeat—and the prices reasonable. The real reasons, of course, are the bridge and poker groups her parents organize with friends and hotel regulars.

Side by side, they walk on the hilly road, lined with hotel and café terraces. In one of the cafés two men play backgammon at a table next to flowering red geraniums. The gray-haired man sets an ashtray on the cement cornice and smokes, nonchalantly pointing his cigarette towards the street, oblivious of the walkers' proximity. The younger one has striking features. Recognizing the boy's father, the girl thinks he has his son's stature, except for the dark eyes and a thin black mustache. He looks at the couple, nods in their direction, waves a hand ready to throw the dice, looks briefly at the girl, his eyes pausing on his son before throwing the dice. "*Shesh besh!*" he says loudly, "I win!"

The boy does not speak, and seems preoccupied.

"He saw us," she says. "What will happen, now?"

"Nothing. My father already talked to me yesterday."

"What did he say?"

"He was very calm about the whole matter. He said it was about time I take my future in hand. Listen. He said exactly these words: 'Who is going to support the two of you? Her family?'"

"That's all he said?"

"That's all."

"I don't understand," she says, frowning.

"My father never talked to me this way. I never thought of marriage before," he says, recalling the worried look on his father's face and the rest of his words: "I have absolutely nothing against this girl. Neither do I really object to the fact that she is Christian, provided, of course, that she embraces our faith. I respect your choice, but the problem is that, at nineteen, you have no job, no career, and you have to think about the girl's reputation."

"Marriage?" she repeats. The sound of this word shakes her; her whole world shatters. Why should they make this decision? she thinks. The sixteen-year-old girl imagines her dreams fast forwarded, full speed on a public screen.

* * *

The mother opens the oven door and bastes the roast for the third time. "I'll be back before it is dry," she thinks. She has to drive her fifteen-year-old son to soccer practice and then pick up the twins from their tennis lesson at the YMCA.

"Let's go, Mom, I'm going to be late again," says her son. He finishes lacing his soccer shoes in the car while she pulls out of the driveway.

She decides to take Crosstown; there will be less traffic at this hour.

"How was your day?" she says, eager to share a few moments of intimacy with her growing son who lately seems always busy doing his homework, watching TV or talking on the phone for hours—that is, when he is not out of the house.

"Fine," he answers. "Everything's fine."

"Do you like your teachers this year?"

"They're OK."

"And what about your classmates? Do you get along with them?" she continues, trying to find something interesting to say.

"Yes. Of course. Why do you keep asking me the same questions every day? We've been going to school a month now, and you keep asking me these same, dumb questions."

"I won't ask you anything anymore," she says, remembering that she has to stop at Jewel's for milk, eggs, and orange juice.

"By the way, Mom, this year there's this Black guy in my class. He made the varsity team with me. He's great. He's really nice. He's different from other Black kids. Can I have him over some day?"

She thinks, "Vinegar, yes, we're out of vinegar and dishwasher liquid, I'll get a head of lettuce and some fruit . . ."

"Mom, can I have him over?"

"Sure, he can come over," she says, watching the road ahead in order to switch into the left lane.

"Great. He's real nice. He lives in a nice neighborhood here in Portage. Can he spend the night?"

"No, just have him come to visit for now. We'll see about spending the night later," she says, her eyes fixed on the road.

"Why can't he sleep over, Mom? He's really nice. You'll see. Is it because he's Black? Tell me."

"I told you he can come. Can't we change the subject?" she replies, irritated.

She thinks of her husband, of what he would have answered. Would he mind?

"Mom, you haven't answered my question. You don't want him to sleep over because he's Black or what?

"No, I have absolutely nothing against Black people, and you know it," she says, imagining the young Black boy at their breakfast table. "Why do you insist on having him sleep over? You can be friends at school, and I told you that he could come some day."

She tries to think of something else, the porch that needs to be painted, the screen door repaired. She does not feel up to arguing. She had always proclaimed her liberal views anyway. She thinks of supper, of the salad she'll have to prepare. "My roast will be burnt if I'm not back on time," she hears herself thinking aloud.

"I hate roasts! Why can't we have something good like spaghetti for a change? Or pizza? Mom, can't you go faster? I'm going to be late."

Cars stop ahead of her, working their way like snails along the dirt road leading to the soccer complex. At her right, some muscular young boys in uniform—some taller, some shorter than her son—are getting out of cars. She glances at him, observing the shadow on his upper lip. He will soon shave, and she will miss his soft baby cheeks.

"Bye, Mom! Pick me up at nine. Not a minute later. I love you," he says, running towards the field.

On the way home, she feels awkward. Her son is at an age at which he is never satisfied with simple answers. "I have never had a Black child at my house before," she thinks. She carries this thought while she shops and picks the twins up. She gets home just in time to salvage her roast. She turns the oven off, covers the Pyrex with aluminum foil, reaches for the place mats and begins to set the table.

* * *

The boy has been patiently waiting for her under a giant oak, at the intersection of Reyfoun and Ajaltoun. She said she knew a place, a secret place she'd show him. She has never been late before, he thinks, and he does not expect her to be late on their first rendezvous away from the rest of the group. He remembers how he and the other boys and girls used to pick her up every day right after the regimented meal hours of summer hotels. She would always be ready, by the main gate, alone or with some friends from the Al Masyaf Hotel. Everything happened so naturally between them. The others were first to notice it and had simply accepted that the two of them would be constantly together.

When the annual series of village dances began, every Saturday at a different café-restaurant in the neighborhood, they never needed to plan anything. They'd get to the café their separate ways with friends, and then, he'd bring a chair and sit next to her. Although he wished they could spend the whole time dancing, he was careful not to raise the entire village's suspicions. Only then, when he began to worry about other people, did he become aware of his feelings towards her.

His previous girlfriends had never meant much to him. Following his older brothers' example, he had proven his virility in brothels—with his father's tacit approval—but had never felt before this summer the intense pleasure experienced in the girl's company. He never tired of listening to her and delighted in watching her almond-shaped eyes sparkle, as if speech were coming out of them. "She is not what's commonly called pretty," he thinks, "yet she has within her the seductiveness of a thousand women." He stretches, feeling her absence, as he looks at his wristwatch.

As he starts to nervously pace the street, she emerges like a sprite from a side-path and runs towards him. "Mother was waiting for me by the bookstore below the hotel," she says. "I said I was meeting Mona and Samia. I know she didn't believe me."

About to say, "Patience is not one of my virtues," he hears himself saying "It's OK. Don't worry about it," already feeling rewarded by her presence.

"Come," she says, "let me show you my secret grotto. We'll be comfortable there in the shade away from everyone. I'll tell you what happened."

She leads the way, across thick vegetation and pine trunks, avoiding thorns and bushes. She stops at times, picks tall stems of flowering oregano, arranges them in a bouquet with dried branches and tiny yellow wildflowers. Their steps crush rusty mounds of dried pine needles echoing the intense cicadas' "Kriss . . . kriss" exacerbated by the midday heat.

"I used to gather thyme every summer for my grand-mother," she says. "She waited for me, smiling, asking for more, always more. She'd dry the leaves, then mix them with different herbs and spices and toasted sesame seeds, making homemade *zaatar*."

Now, they walk hand in hand. He watches her, amused, as she still gathers wild branches with her free hand, pulling him down-wards with each movement. "I used to make necklaces out of pine needles" she says, "and bracelets also. Did you ever do that?"

"No. I always preferred the sea to the mountain. I liked fishing, collecting seashells. I still have a nice collection."

"You must have carved pipes from acorns; all boys do this. I loved their fuzzy centers. You know, like artichokes.'"

"I don't remember," he says, absentmindedly.

As they leave the pine forest, the landscape changes drastically. They climb over boulders partially covered with dried grass, thistles and thorns. They work their way up, silently, using hands and knees at times, avoiding brambles, trying to follow goat trails as much as possible.

"Here it is," she says, pointing at a gaping opening in the rocky wall above them.

"What brought you here, the first time?"

"I discovered the grotto two years ago, hiking with my friends Paul and Fady. We were exploring the mountain for hiding places."

* * *

Sunday afternoon, upon leaving the Crossroads Mall, at about four o'clock, she sees her son biking with a Black boy about the same age.

"Hi, Mom. This is Kevin."

"Hi, Kevin," she says. His smile seems to come through his eyes, illuminating his whole face. She stares until he stops smiling, embarrassed.

"Don't be late for supper," she says, hurrying to the car.

"I may go to the movies with Kevin, Mom. I'll call you."

On the way home she thinks of Howard's smile. She has just seen a younger version of Howard. Yet with different features. Howard. She has not thought of him in such a long time. All she can recall now is his smile, brightening his face, his eyes. His smile which always made everything seem easy, even possible back then, during her college years when Howard was in her psychology classes. He was Black, and she considered him her best friend. They used to walk together every day to class and talk, just about everything. She thought he felt something for her for a while, but nothing ever happened between them. It seems so long ago. She almost takes a wrong turn, realizes it on time and switches back into the middle lane.

She tries to keep her mind on the road, but thinking of Howard makes her think of Mike and Marguerite. Mike was her brother's best friend. He had been going out with a Senegalese girl Marguerite for over four years. They were law students and got along so well that the news of their marriage would not have surprised anyone, until they broke up for some unknown reason. She remembers the long evenings Mike spent at their home talking about Marguerite. No one really understood what had gone wrong, but his parents considered themselves blessed that the relationship had ended. "It seems so long ago," she thinks, realizing that she has not thought of them for ages. She could never forget Mike's expression when he said that he could only make love to a Black woman, praising Marguerite's dark skin, so perfect. He once said "There is something mysterious about black skin, the sort of thing which makes a work of art, a statue out of a human body, erasing from one's thought, veins, freckles, spots and other imperfections. On a black skin, you forget the inside of the body."

She has never realized before this minute, how well engraved Mike's words had been on her seventeen-year-old mind. The last time she saw Mike was years ago, in Toledo, Ohio—shortly after her marriage. Her brother had organized a family reunion, and Mike happened to be visiting him at the same time. Why would it all suddenly come back after seeing

Kevin and her son together? Opening the door to her house, she is struck by the silence, then remembers that her husband and the twins had gone to the movies while she was shopping, and would be back soon for supper. In her room, she takes off her dress, slips into a comfortable jumpsuit, her favorite slippers, and goes to the kitchen. She takes the marinated chicken, the lettuce and some tomatoes out of the refrigerator. After slicing the tomatoes, she reaches down in the lazy Susan for a red onion.

Her husband always likes onions in the salad, and she tries not to forget it. Her husband's comments on the Mike-Marguerite affair come to her mind. He had met Mike at the reunion in Toledo, and when he heard about his relationship with Marguerite, he had said without the least hesitation "I don't understand Mike, at all. To me, a Black woman is unappealing. I could never make love to a Black woman. Never." His grimace of disgust made her feel uneasy. She was not particularly attracted to Black men, but she did not find them unattractive either. "It depends," she thinks. "It's hard to generalize." And now, Howard's face, his smile, keeps coming back to her mind insistently, mixed with Kevin's smile. Would she have brought up Howard in that discussion, back then? She can't remember the rest of their conversation. Had she finally decided to keep her thoughts on this subject to herself, or had she explained that she found some Black men attractive and ended up arguing with him? Because this had been the pattern in their relationship all along; she had grown accustomed to listening to her husband and agreeing, or else she was accused of always looking for a fight. She had avoided open discussions for so long, that she now thought: "Not only do I no longer know what my husband really thinks, but I'm not sure of my own convictions anymore."

She remembers Kevin and her son on their bikes. They must be at the movies, now. Would her husband object to his presence in the house? Both of them had openly expressed their views about equality between races. She had often heard him talk in these terms to the children. "There should be no problem," she decides. She seasons her salad and sprinkles lemon and salt over the chicken.

* * *

The grotto, as the girl calls it, looks like an accident in the sur-rounding greenness. Carved by man or nature, in the steep side of the mountain overlooking the sea, this small cave can only be reached from one direction. Wide enough for two couples at the most, its walls' and ceiling's porous surface is covered with inscriptions, hearts and initials.

"I think it must have been the refuge of all the lovers in the area for generations," she says, feeling the soft rose-colored walls with her fingers. She rubs her palms against each other, enjoying the silky texture of the pastel powder coming out of the walls.

"What do you think?" she asks, running her fingers once more over the smooth surface.

"Perhaps. Let's take a look at the dates. They're not that old. Here's 1927? And 1970, see, here, 1962. Someone came here not too long ago. It seems that a key or a bobby pin would cut into these walls. I wonder what they're made of?"

"It must have been in a similar cave that Khalil Gibran used to meet his married lady in Besharri."

"It was not a cave, but a forgotten temple carved in the rock where lovers used to hide back then. I've been there once on my way to the Cedars. Have you ever visited Gibran's house and seen his paintings? It is worth seeing."

"I saw his house, but not the temple," she answers. "I've read his stories about Selma, their pure, impossible love, and how they talked at length, and read poetry. Did you know he took along a book of Andalusian poems? I wonder what the temple is like."

"It has ancient carvings of the Love Goddess, Ishtar, on one side, and more modern fifteenth century carvings of Christ on the cross on the other side. It seems ideal for a mystic's love. No?" he adds, laughing and holding her tight.

"I like to think that we are in a similar cave," she says, pressing herself against him as they sit on the edge of the cave their feet dangling in the void. She feels her whole body emptying, wishes his presence would fill it, keeping her from flying, soaring in the air above, up north, above, above Besharri, the Cedars, until she could see all the mountains of Lebanon as from an airplane. His arms and lips ground her, keep her from falling over slopes, precipices, crevices, the way a huge rock would, rumbling down, quickly, two thousand meters below into the blue sea.

They look at the deep blue lining the far horizon, then penetrating and wavering into the turquoise waters of the Jounieh Bay without mixing, as if the two liquids were of different densities. From this distance, the clear bay resembles a transparent pool. No red-roof tiles are in sight over the green slopes. There are no houses nearby.

"We're going back to Beirut soon. School starts in three weeks."

"We'll stay a little longer," he replies. "In Tyre they start a week later."

"My mother does not want me to see you ever again" she says, not knowing if that is why she is sad, or if it is because even without her mother's intervention, going back to Beirut represents a separation anyway.

"We'll write, and I'll come to see you during Christmas. I have a married sister who lives in Beirut. We get along very well. She will help us."

He holds her tight, and she forgets the village, her parents, the fact that he is Muslim. She sees his green eyes through her closed eyelids, thinks of his tanned skin she noticed on the first day they met. It made her think of apricots. Later, he explained it was his natural color. He did not get much darker from the sun.

They stop kissing as if the inscriptions around them were a million eyes, peering at them. She searches for his hand and thinks of her mother.

* * *

She decides to take a brisk walk before she showers and dresses. She has done enough housework for today she thinks, and feels like exploring the neighborhood on this sunny October morning. She marvels at the clusters of red leaves here and there, at some completely yellow trees losing their drying leaves while some others remain green and intact. Autumn is definitely her favorite season, but, unfortunately, the colors never last long enough. She likes to go out as much as possible at this time of the year, delighting in the unexpected changes of the surrounding vegetation, trying very hard to preserve the vivid colors in her mind during the long, predictable winter. Her son has been asking again about inviting Kevin over and she has agreed. "It is not important," she thinks. Yet, she feels uneasy every time she thinks of the two boys together.

After a quick, invigorating shower, during which she imagines she is an autumn tree losing its multicolored leaves under a ruthless storm, she decides to wear her gray suit. She is meeting her friend Betty for lunch; they have decided to take time off, now that the children are back in school.

While they eat their salads, she finds herself asking Betty, "Do your children have Black friends?"

"Sure, they do," Betty says. "Why?"

"It is not really important. Do your children invite them to your house?"

"I don't know. I mean yes, they do," says Betty, with an amused smile.

"Do they sleep over?"

"I don't understand what you're getting at," replies Betty. "I don't remember exactly. But, yes, once in a while. My children don't have a very close friend who is Black. I mean, there isn't a kid hanging around my house all the time if that's what you mean. Since when have you been interested in racial problems?"

"Honestly, I don't know myself. My son has a new friend at school, a Black boy, and he keeps talking about having him over. I have never had a Black child in my house before, you know."

She feels stupid to have brought up the subject with Betty today, but Betty is not going to let go that easily.

"What are you concerned about?" says Betty, wiping her lips delicately with her napkin. "Are you afraid you are a racist?"

She hoped Betty would not say that word. She hates racists. She certainly is not one.

"No," she says, "the thought has not even crossed my mind. I have nothing against mixed marriages, either. I only think that the couple is heading for more problems, and that it must be rough on the children. But . . . me, a racist? It has never even been an issue for me. The truth is that it is my husband's opinions, which preoccupy me. I don't know what he really thinks; I mean deep down. I wonder how he would react to a new Black friend."

She finishes her wine, then adds: "Betty, I think that what bothers me is that I have acted strangely with my son. I don't want him to get the feeling that I discriminate on grounds of race, because I don't. Let me tell you about a couple that I've known well."

"Let's have coffee at my house," says Betty.

* * *

Her head against his chest, the girl remembers her excitement, earlier in the day, at the thought of meeting him alone and going to the grotto. She vaguely remembers the conversation with her mother and sister during lunch; her main concern was to leave unnoticed. After lunch, the hotel guests spread out in corners, coffee cups in hand in the living room or towards one of the many terraces surrounding the building. The girl, who had been allowed to drink the strong Turkish coffee for the second year now, never missed the opportunity to swallow the black concoction which made her feel part of the adult world.

She left her mother comfortably seated on a sofa with another lady and slipped into her room. She took great care in setting her hair, and after a long hesitation, decided to wear her blue cotton shirt. She wore some of her older sister's perfume and happily left the slumbering hotel. Soon, she thought, everyone will be resting, sleeping or reading as usual. Her mother always did. No one would notice her absence; of this she was absolutely certain.

At the bottom of the steep serpentine road, half a mile away from the hotel, she turned right towards the bookstore and the candy stand across the street from the Cocorico café. Her mother was there, stern, standing in her high heels, magazines rolled in her fist like a weapon.

"Where do you think you are going?" she said, her lips pinched, her eyes, severe.

"I'm going to see Mona and Samia."

"Mona and Samia, eh? And who else? The rest of the clique?"

She did not answer.

"How can you be so thoughtless and irresponsible!" exploded her mother. "I should never have allowed you to go out with this group in the first place. I knew from the very first day I saw that boy that he meant trouble. I knew it the very first time he came to the hotel with the others. I should have reacted then, right from the start."

The girl recalled the first day he came to the hotel. His tall, distinguished silhouette, his green eyes, his innate charm. She fought back: "His older brother has been part of Mireille's group for over two years now, and you never objected. Why me? Everything I do is wrong in your eyes!"

"Your sister did not do anything behind my back," her mother said, "Like walk hand in hand all over the village. Or did you think I'd never know? How do you think I felt when some ladies at the hotel told me kindly that my daughter is in love with a Muslim? What do you think they think? That I haven't brought you up properly!"

She paused for a minute, then continued, "What are you after? A scandal? Be grateful that your father has been too preoccupied with his business to have noticed anything."

She stopped talking, then nodded, as if talking to herself, withdrawn in her own thoughts.

"If I could convince your father, I would not stay here one day longer. We would all go to the other end of Lebanon, to another resort village, and spend the rest of the summer there. But I can't find a good reason to take you away from here. You must promise me you won't see him again," her mother said raising her tone.

"I can't. He's in the group. There's nothing between us anyway. Nothing to worry about. Mom, I'm late. People are watching us. I have to go."

"You won't make this promise?" pleaded her mother. "If only your father gets to know this! I can't watch you every minute of the day like when you were a child. Listen to me. This is wrong."

* * *

"Just right!" she says, turning off the burner from under the sizzling pan. She divides the bacon strips into three equal shares, butters the toasts and stirs the orange juice between sips of her morning coffee. Her husband has already gone to work. Up before dawn, he never eats breakfast. He usually takes some fruit during his nine o'clock coffee break at the fermentation plant, where he has to arrive early to supervise the experiments. She pours orange juice in the glasses and gets the milk out of the refrigerator. The night before, she had a dream and she could remember every detail up until this second. The dream had something to do with her brother and his friend Mike. They were having a wild party in somebody's beach house, but that was all she could remember. The memory of Mike brought the image of Marguerite. Who knows where she is today? "Probably back in Senegal and married to a lawyer or a diplomat maybe with a bunch of Black kids," she thinks. Perhaps she was better off not to have married Mike. She imagines Mike and Marguerite with Black children with curly blond hair and light eyes.

Her three children are eating their eggs silently when her older son says, "Mom, is it all right if Kevin comes today after school?"

"No, today is not a good day. I have nothing planned for supper. Tomorrow is fine. I'll make spaghetti and meatballs and we'll have garlic bread. How does that sound?"

"Fine. I'll see if he can make it. Bye, Mom."

"Bye, Mommy! Bye!" say the twins, always full of energy, waving to her from the street.

Thinking of Mike and Marguerite makes her reflect upon her own marriage. She wonders if difficulties always sustain a great passion. She wonders if her husband has ever loved her as Mike loved Marguerite. She hurries and cleans the kitchen. She has an aerobic class at eleven, and wants to get the ironing done by then.

While ironing her husband's shirts, she thinks of how dependent men are on their wives' daily actions. She feels the intimacy of pressing beneath the fabric of the neckline, the arms, the chest. She senses her husband's presence with every shirt she hangs and experiences a strong sense of closeness and pride. "Too bad he does not share it," she thinks. But men don't think of these things. They don't have time. Or are men less sensitive than women? Some are different, though. The first to come to her mind is Howard. Yes, he was very sensitive. Anyway she has never mentioned him to her husband. Why should she? After all, they were only friends. Besides, her husband was so possessive that she barely mentioned her previous boyfriends or first loves. He would not understand. Yet, she had experienced a great intimacy with Howard. They could talk for hours, back then. She probably talked more with him than with her husband after all these years of marriage, she reflects, spraying some more starch over the collar's stubborn wrinkles, the way her mother always did.

She remembers her mother's words. "People are all equal, but different. Each one should remain with his own," her mother often repeated sententiously, pointing her index finger to the ceiling. "You can have friends, but keep your distances! Keep your distances!" She wonders what her mother would have thought had she known of her friendship with Howard. Her father had died shortly after she went to college, but he was a quiet and melancholic man who always relied on his wife to make most of the decisions, especially around the house. Her mother was extremely opposed to Mike's love for Marguerite and never made a secret of it, always lecturing her children: "That's the best thing that could have happened to Mike. He does not know how lucky he is they broke up. God loves him! And his parents! Not that I have anything against Marguerite, but, each with his own kind! Keep your distances!" Of what her husband really thought about the whole issue, she is no longer sure, she reflects as she puts the iron on its stand and unplugs it.

* * *

"You must send his letters back and ask him for yours!" her mother says. "Things are worse than I had expected! So, this boy is planning on coming to Beirut for Christmas, now! Fool! What do you think will happen? He does not care. He'll marry you, and then, later, when he is tired of you, he'll get a younger one. And you, you would have denied your faith, not the other way around. Can you imagine? Be excommunicated! You would be a pariah, never accepted by them. Nobody really respects someone who rejects his faith. You'd lose your friends, your family. And most of all, you'd bring Muslim children into the world! Have you thought of that? Holy Virgin!"

Her mother's voice breaks. Her eyes, naturally round, pop out like glass eyes. "I have never seen her this way," thinks the girl, crying silently. Ever since she and her family came down from the mountains she has tried to hide her feelings from her sister. She could not stop crying some nights and feared her sister would wake up. And now, her mother has read her letters, a thing the girl thought was sacred. Years ago, her mother had given her a portable secretary. It was made of carved, polished wood. "I got it for a present when I was your age," she had said. "I'd like you to have it." She enjoyed its secret drawers and green felt writing pad. Her sister did not know the intricate mechanism that opened them, and she never thought her mother would pry into her personal papers. She had been saving her most intimate thoughts in these drawers, and now, his letters.

"You ignored my warnings. Things have gone too far!" says the mother, pacing the room.

"But, Mother, I love him. We love . . ."

"Love!" explodes the mother. "This word is good for movies or novels. There is nothing sensible based on love. Certainly not one single marriage! And to love a Muslim! Good Lord! What have I done to be punished this way? I can't believe that we kept the whole matter from your father! God prevents me from even imagining his reaction. He would lock you up in a boarding school at the very least. If he knew you had been hiding in grottos in the wilderness, kissing a Muslim, and God knows what! Holy Virgin! Jesus, help me! How did all this come to pass?"

She has definitely read all my letters, thinks the girl, unable to think about anything else. . . . All my letters, my thoughts.

"Don't you have pride? Nor self respect?" continues the mother, unleashed. "Let yourself be kissed by a Muslim, let him use you, touch you, knowing he thinks you're trash for being so easy!"

"It was not like that!" bursts the girl. "It's not true. He is not at all like this. I love him. We only kissed, that's all."

"Let us hope there is still time to correct the situation. You are going to write to him right now, and from now on you will not take a step out of this house without me. This must end today without your father ever finding out."

The girl goes to her room and sits at her desk. She takes out a few sheets of writing paper and thinks of him—smiling, confident they will see each other again. She starts writing the date, slowly, wondering what she can tell him, then starts scribbling automatically, drawing curves and parallel lines careful not to let the lines overlap until the whole page is covered with intricate designs.

She tries to imagine his disappointment when he gets her letter. Will he understand the extent of her pain? She keeps drawing on the page, writing his name, their initials, and crosses them out right away, remembering the grotto's porous surface. She presses the paper with her pen. . . . It cannot penetrate. She presses harder, imagining she is carving over the walls of the cave. She thinks of the softness of the powder that came off those walls, of the softness of his skin and lips.

She tears the page, wrinkles it and throws it into the trash-can. Then, writing the date on top of a clean page, she feels his green eyes staring at her. He had Christmas vacation all planned. They'd see each other every day. It was too good to be true. They could run away, fight, work their way through. Others had done it. No one could make her change her faith. But the children would have to be Muslim. Could she live with that? She hides her face wet with tears in her hands. She starts writing, his green eyes staring at her through the page.

* * *

She smoothes the meatballs between her palms, moistening her hands from time to time under the running tap. Then, she sautés them, constantly shaking the frying pan in a circular motion, allowing them to brown evenly. "I'll add the tomato sauce later when I boil the spaghetti," she thinks and decides to take a break while she still has the house to herself. She scrubs her hands energetically, several times, to rid her skin of the particles adhering under her nails, all around her cuticles and of the smell of onions and raw meat.

She sets the teakettle on the stove, and watches her lobelias and dusty millers through her window, still vigorous despite the change of weather. "My lobelias turned out to be purple this year, like violets," she thinks. She had written a research paper once about the symbolism of colors and flowers. Howard had read it and discussed it with her. Green was soothing to people, this she remembers. There was something about black roses. Black always interested Howard, of course; he always connected everything to African studies.

"Howard was a good man," she thinks, wondering where he is now; probably happily married. At least making a woman very happy. She remembers when he dated Elizabeth, a plump redhead, and she missed their walks together. She felt some sort of jealousy deep inside when she saw them side-by-side.

Her son said that Kevin would ride the bus with him from school. She recalls the image of the two boys riding bikes outside the mall the previous Sunday, as she prepares an infusion of Earl Grey leaves. She can't help thinking of Sandeep, her son's Indian friend, with whom he constantly roamed the streets. She never questioned their friendship. Neither did her husband. She had gotten to know Sandeep's mother with whom she got along pretty well and who taught her the secrets and rituals of Indian tea.

As she pours herself a second cup of tea, she hears noise coming from the garage. Then, in a flash, a four-headed mass of limbs tries to make its way through the kitchen door at the same time. "Hi, Mommy! Hi, Mom! Hi Ma'am!" "Hey guys, let's shoot some baskets!" Within seconds, book bags are all over the floor, and the boys vanish towards the yard. She brings the thick tomato sauce to a boil and adds the meatballs, watching them sink, one by one. She then covers the pan and reduces the heat to simmer. While cleaning the counters, she hears her husband's car pulling in the garage.

"Hi, honey!" he says, kissing her cheek as she wipes the ceramic sink. "I see we have company. New friend, eh?"

"Yes."

"We had some visitors from Germany who studied the plant from top to bottom today. I have a strange taste in my throat. It's these fermentation fumes! I tell you, these bacteria release chemicals and God knows what!"

She imagines him all impregnated with the fermentation fumes, as if these substances could penetrate deep inside him through his clothes and skin, altering his blood, mind and thoughts. She follows him to their bedroom and watches him draw the water and undress, neatly piling his clothes in a corner of the bathroom.

"The boy's name is Kevin. Our son is very fond of him. He has been wanting to have him over for some time, now," she says.

He reaches for a towel from the bathroom closet and places it above the toilet seat.

"He wanted Kevin to sleep over," she adds.

"Fine," he says, entering the half-empty tub and sinking into it, eager to feel the comfort of warm water. "It's so good," he says, his eyes half-closed. She sits sideways on the edge of the tub and hands him a large bar of soap.

"So, you would not mind if our son had a Black friend?"

"Mind?" he says, turning the faucet to set the water's temperature on hot. "My secretary is Black!"

So, his secretary is Black, she thinks as she watches the vapor rise, fogging the bathroom mirror, and at the same time hears him say, "Only make sure you don't make a habit of it. Everything has its limits."

"I have to boil the water for the spaghetti," she says, getting up and leaving the bathroom.

From the kitchen window she stares at the children playing around the basketball hoop and adds a handful of coarse salt to the water. The children's voices are getting louder and louder. She imagines that all four children could very well have been hers, and she suddenly feels extremely tired.

She stirs the spaghetti in the bubbling water and watches the reflection of her back window in the microwave oven door above the range. The steam rises in wavy columns as if blown over the smooth, black surface, blurring her vision, creating purple and green iridescence striping the oven door.

The door sweats with the constant rise of steam. Now the children's play seems more distant in the backyard. Stirring frequently, she watches condensed droplets form, merge and drip into broken, irregular lines, the way they are dripping at the same moment over their bathroom mirror, fogging her husband's image, erasing details, shapes, colors, the way they could very well be dripping somewhere else at the same moment over another bathroom mirror, over Howard's image. . . .

BY FIRE OR WATER

It was one of those old houses that must have been deep pink once, with coral wrought iron over the balustrades and under the half-opened red shutters. The sepia walls were discolored in places—unprotected for years from the sun and the corroding coastal mist. Here and there thin layers of plaster were peeling off, reminding me of the heavily sunburned backs frequently seen along the beaches.

In spite of the heat an incredibly long line had already formed at nine in the morning, extending all around the house, so that we would have to do a full turn before reaching the entrance again. Two broad shouldered men guarded the main gate: One of them, almost an albino, had curly whitish hair and pink rabbit eyes; the other was tanned, his luminous green eyes framed with thick frowning eyebrows.

These guards and the crowd seemed out of place around the isolated house; so close to the shore the rising tides must be a menace. I watched foamy waves explode against the rocks and disappear in a faint roar, smearing the sand with salty scum. The waves' incessant flux, a soothing palm over the burning sand, polished its surface, leaving it smooth and shiny—except for the bulging shells resisting the water's suction. Unlike the layers of fine sand gradually vanishing after each stroke, the shells' irregular shapes remained encrusted in the compact shore, crested for a brief moment with iridescent bubbles.

We walked silently, until we found ourselves in front of the main gate. After we crossed the garden, behind a half-opened arched door, a tiny old woman smiled at us with carmine painted lips. Her shiny henna-colored hair, coiled in a perfect chignon, clashed with a wrinkled face streaked like a shattered windshield. She led us into a waiting room, dark and cool as a natural cave, the half-closed shutters retaining the humidity. When my eyes adjusted to the semi-darkness, I discerned folding chairs, naked walls, faces, feet resting on straw floor-mats. I liked this tinted atmosphere. I felt I was entering a picture dyed in strong tea.

We sat down in a corner next to an old man, head bent, rolling his rosary beads between his fingers. Opposite us, a woman seated on the straw mat nursed her baby, covering her breast with a big handkerchief. She wiped the baby's mouth, then, discretely offered him her other breast.

"I wonder what these people are here for," Naila said. I looked at her as if seeing her for the first time. Nothing in her personality indicated that she would ever turn to occult powers. She was always so perfect, so sure of herself. Why couldn't she see the contradiction between this visit and her strong religious beliefs?

We were both educated in Catholic convent schools. Naila had always intimidated me with her self-righteous attitude. I wondered how she had convinced me to accompany her to Fatma's faded sepia house. Six months had passed since Khalil had returned from Lyon. Six months since he broke up with her.

I knew what she was going through under her apparent detachment, behind the serene smile that characterized her.

Everyone in Beirut had heard of Fatma whose popularity had increased lately, even among other medical students. Every day we would hear that so and so in school had seen Fatma. Visiting her had become a fad. Yet, it still felt awkward—two years before graduation—waiting to see Fatma in this old house.

"I've heard that Fatma is a multi-millionaire," I said. "She certainly doesn't keep her house well."

"Do you think she lives here? It could be her work place."

"Maybe. Something grabs me about this old sepia house—neglected as it is."

"Tania, have you made up your mind about . . ."

"No."

"You could ask her about Mounir," she said with her enigmatic smile.

"Please. I don't want to talk about him. He's married and has a daughter. What good will it do to relive the whole thing?"

I resented her reminding me of Mounir. It was hard enough to put up with her constant "Is it possible Khalil never really loved me?"

"Do you think he has someone else?" she asked, staring at me the same way she did whenever unable to solve a clinical problem. "Do as you will, Tania. I want to know as much as I can about Khalil and me. I know I'm acting funny, but I can't help it." Immediately, she raised her eyebrows, signaling with her chin in the direction of the door, "Look! Here comes the painted corpse."

The old woman checked everyone's number, each time twitching her carmine lips in a nervous tic. As I handed her our cards, she stared at us and asked, "You two are together? Follow me."

She preceded us into a dark red-tiled hallway. We passed closed doors. The third door was open, and she invited us inside. It was a replica of the first room: same tinted atmosphere, people seated on folding chairs, straw floor-mats all over.

In the quietness of this room, I sensed the nearby sea humming its fading call and I wished we were lying on the beach instead of sitting here like uneducated, credulous people. It all seemed a waste of time when we only had a few days break before our externship.

What would I ask Fatma? I could not deny a certain fascination for the mystery that lies beyond rational thought. Consulting a seer had never crossed my mind when Mounir and I broke up. Yet, would Naila have accompanied me? I imagined her reaction, her "Come on! You can't be serious." All she did at the time was repeat, "You'll get over it, Tania. Mounir wasn't good enough for you. He isn't worth feeling sorry about," as if she knew what was good for me. As if she knew.

Now, an absent look to her face, she was frantically picking her nails as she usually did when we studied for a test—I smoked while she picked her nails. Mounir kept trying to make me quit. When we stopped seeing each other, I locked myself up in my room and smoked cigarette after cigarette, reading aloud all my textbooks; these were the only moments I did not cry. After months and months going through an infinite number of Gitanes blue packs, my voice turned raucous. I feared my vocal chords were broken—the only tangible evidence of Mounir's passage in my life.

Unable to read aloud anymore, I had to reduce the number of cigarettes. It took me a long while to recover and only these past months had my voice become normal again. I looked at Naila; she definitely had her questions ready. I did not think she was after a miracle or that she was deeply convinced of finding an answer here. No. She just sought opportunities to talk about Khalil.

"Tania, I'm going to work on these forms a while. I'll have to drop them at the St. George's hospital this afternoon."

I watched her form perfect letters. She was the only one in class who took readable notes. My friends often told me that parts of my writing were indecipherable. It must have helped Naila to have such a beautiful handwriting when she corresponded with Khalil, when he was away, studying in Lyon. Four years of separation! I always thought theirs was an epistolary affair. I never believed it would work. It took Mounir and I a couple of months away from one another, and we broke up, settling it in one summer.

I never believed that Naila and Khalil wrote each other weekly, either—What is there to write about every week?—until that day when she showed me four thick folders, one for each year. His letters, I glimpsed, were brief; his handwriting as nice as hers. I had never seen anything like it. They were too orderly for my taste, too perfect, like everything she did. I had imagined over the years her relationship as a pasteurized, controlled passion. I could see medical files in place of her folders.

I had always dreamed of love letters delicately laced with endless curls of satin pastel ribbons, hidden in secret drawers or thrown pell-mell in forgotten old trunks, among faded photographs and worn out lace. Nothing like our few letters: hot or cold, endless or laconic. Mounir and I had agreed to exchange our letters and destroy them right away. I did not even keep his picture.

Naila had acted so superior then. She tried to comfort me with her eternal, "He was not good enough for you," or "I often

91

told you he wasn't mature," alluding to the fact that Mounir and I were the same age. She viewed her relationship as perfect: Khalil knew what he was doing; he was five years older.

I sensed some agitation around me and vaguely noticed feet moving, pacing the straw mats. Next to Naila, two middle-aged women were speaking simultaneously to each other while looking in the direction of the door. Naila seemed like a child asking her mother to put a band-aid on a bleeding finger. Now, the pain was deeper—Khalil had disappeared from her life.

For me, breaking up with Mounir had been a turning point. When I ceased to believe in him, nothing else mattered. I had often thought that only people in love knew what it was like to believe in God. Maybe love was godliness. Undoubtedly, Naila would consider these thoughts blasphemous.

I remembered the times when Khalil would return to Beirut for summer vacation; Naila would vanish completely, afraid we would steal him away from her, not wanting to lose a single minute of their time together. I always thought of her as being on a shelf, missing the best moments, refusing to go out all year long. Mounir and I had a few good years together. Nothing is meant to last; what would life be in an eternal Eden? As boring, I thought, as Naila's four folders.

Naila was staring passively at the people around us, eyelids slightly lowered. Her eyes brightened as the old woman entered. "I was beginning to think that they had forgotten about us," she said.

"Now we'll see Fatma, at last," I said, following the woman through another open door. But no. She signaled us to sit down in another waiting room, identical to the others, maybe smaller.

"When are we going to see Fatma?" I asked.

"Your turn is coming shortly," the carmine lips smiled, uncovering yellow teeth smeared with lipstick.

"At least we're not waiting under the sun. It must be hell outside by now," I said. "I only wish we could get some coffee."

"Have you thought of something?"

"Yes. I'll ask her about Sami. I really think I'm falling in love with him. Did I tell you I have been working in his section for a month? He recently was appointed chief obstetrician at the Maternité Française. Every time I walk by his office, my heart beats like a teenager's. Isn't that funny?"

Naila was smiling, a mixture of indifference and interest in her eyes. I continued, "I have always liked him, but I think he only considers me a friend. I can't figure him out. Anyway, that's all I can think of asking right now. I haven't lost a ring like your cousin."

"Isn't that story incredible?" Naila said, stressing each syllable. "That diamond cost a fortune. And to think it was hidden in the maid's cupboard, in Mary's own house. Luckily, she asked Fatma before the maid had a chance to dispose of it." When Naila smiled, her whole face smiled as well. Her tiny eyes disappeared, making it impossible to know what she was thinking because she also smiled when she cried.

"I'm afraid of what Fatma will tell me," she said. "I feel I'm doing something wrong. I could be entering Khalil's consciousness. I'm not sure I'd like that."

"Don't take it so seriously. She's not an infallible oracle, you know. She'll probably read what's in your mind. That's all there is to it!"

"That's all?"

"It's a lot. Don't you think? Consider that Fatma is illiterate and a former maid. I admit I'm in a hurry to get out of here myself."

It must be so hard for Naila to accept that Khalil has stopped loving her, I thought, that she would rather be told impossible "revelations" to avoid facing this simple reality. It was hard for me also. Three years of my life disappearing one summer like a spider-web removed with one finger. As a child, I often marveled at spider-webs, especially at the ones I'd find on bushes when the morning mist glittered under the sun's rays. I played at destroying their fragile texture.

I closed my eyes. Mounir. I had to turn my face away every time I saw couples kissing or holding hands.

"Finally!" Naila said. I opened my eyes and saw the tiny old woman approach. She took us through another red-tiled corridor, then up a long spiral staircase, then into another room on the second floor full of seated people. This time, instead of folding chairs, couches leaned against the naked walls.

"Is this the last one?" Naila asked, "are there more rooms?"

"This is the last stop," said our guide with a satisfied, professional look, as if she had never done anything else in her whole life but lead people from one room to another.

"Tania, I've never told you Mona's story," said Naila in a hushed voice, after the woman left. "She's one of my mother's friends from Tyre. She was extremely ill with severe cramps in her stomach for three years, and no doctor could find a physiological cause for her symptoms. Her health was deteriorating, and she lived on tranquilizers and painkillers. One day, a friend of hers recommended that she should come to Beirut to see Fatma."

"And?"

"Fatma told her that the old cook, who had been in their family for years, and whom she had fired because he was becoming too bossy, had cast an evil spell on her. Fatma said that she could undo that spell which was causing the pains. Mona was told to get special permission to dig up a specific grave. As you can imagine, although Mona's husband is influential in Tyre, it was not easy to obtain this permission. In short, Fatma went with Mona and they found a nail piercing the cadaver's navel. Around the nail was rolled a folded piece of cloth covered with talismanic writings and figures, containing what appeared to be strands of Mona's hair. Her husband demanded a lab analysis. It was her hair. After that day, Mona's pain disappeared."

I was beginning to have goose bumps. I definitely would rather be out in the sun, looking at the blue sea nearby, walking barefoot along the wet shoreline. I tried to tell myself that Mona's story could be a tale after all. No one could have such powers. Telepathy . . . yes, but the rest, doubtful. We both remained silent.

Would Fatma have a crystal ball, burning incense, a red or green scarf around her head, a bright-colored shawl thrown over her gathered long skirt? A gypsy? No, of course not, there are no gypsies in Lebanon. She'd be wearing a long black dress like some village women. A long black dress, her head covered with a black veil. Or maybe she'd be sitting on the floor, in the lotus position, smoking a *narguileh*, sorting out a deck of playing cards or Tarot.

"Who's first?" asked the little old woman as if coming from nowhere.

"Can't we go together?" I asked.

"Why don't you go first?" said Naila, her whole face smiling apprehensively.

An ordinary, middle-aged woman in a lilac shirt-dress welcomed me, "*Marhaba!*"

"*Marhaba*," I answered. She was sitting on a wooden chair, by a wooden table with a notebook, a pencil in her raised right hand, in the perfect composure of a schoolteacher about to give an oral test. It made me more nervous. I always hated orals.

"Sit down," Fatma said.

I sat down on the chair facing her in the middle of this barren room. I noticed a sink behind a curtain, and a little gas burner on which a small coffee pot was trembling.

"Would you like some coffee? It's ready," she offered.

"Yes, *shoukran*."

Fatma poured the boiling coffee into a tiny cup with a narrow base, similar to the ones I'd seen Bedouins use at Ba'albeck's last festival. She could have passed unnoticed in the street or in a supermarket. She wore her black hair short, around an insignificant oval face. Her eyes were an impossible cross between molten lead and the unquiet softness of a fawn's restless eyes. She tore a sheet from the notebook, centered it on the table, and paused until I'd emptied my cup.

I watched her place a coffee cup containing a shiny oily liquid in the center of her palm. She raised her hand obliquely, stared at the oil, as her five fingers delicately moved the cup in a circular motion.

"Concentrate," she ordered. "Close your eyes."

"Open your eyes, now." My eyes followed her pencil's movements on the page. She was writing "Sami" in Arabic, letter by letter as if she were transcribing individual messages from the bottom of the cup. It's impossible. I didn't even have time enough to think of him.

"What is it you want to know about him?"

"I . . . I wanted to know if he is serious. I mean, if he is interested in me." She must have thought I was stupid.

She covered her intense eyes with her palms for a second, scrutinized the cup once more, then said, "He is flirting. He is not serious. Anything else you want to know?"

"No, *shoukran*." I found it hard to stand up. It seemed it'd been ages.

"*Shoukran*," I repeated, as Naila entered. The old woman showed me the way out through the dark, narrow red-tiled corridors. The waiting rooms were packed. I emerged like a scared hermit crab forced to abandon his shell, dazzled by the blinding light and the impossible heat. I paced the street, my eyes fixed on the rusty wrought-iron gate, waiting for Naila. I hoped the visits were timed, because she could stay in there for hours talking about her Khalil. Despite the sweat dripping all over me, even behind my kneecaps, I felt free. I could stretch my limbs and my mind after hours of immobility and expectation. The line was unbelievably long and dense. At last, I saw Naila running out of the sepia house.

"What did she tell you?" she asked with a smile.

"Not much. She said that Sami wasn't serious about me. And you?"

"She said there was a deed—a kind of curse, or spell, cast against me by some of Khalil's relatives to separate us. She could not specify how close they were to him."

"And?"

"She said she could undo it."

"She can?"

"Yes."

"Do you believe it?"

"I'm not taking a chance. I'll have to come back with a hundred pounds and a small piece of material cut from a bra or a slip. It doesn't matter, as long as it is something I have worn often. She said she'd take care of the whole matter and give me a talisman against the deed."

"Another day like this one! What if she told you this only to extort more money from you?" I said without the slightest conviction. Despite my attempt to rationalize, I still saw Fatma's pencil moving in her fingers as if it were alive, tracing the letters s-a-m-i on the page.

"No. No," she said, "I won't even stand in line. The old woman is instructed to take both the piece of material and the money from me. Fatma gave me a note to the gate guardians. It's all so strange. I don't feel I'm the same person anymore. It's already one o'clock! I'd better run. I'll call you soon. Bye!"

* * *

After the visit to Fatma's house, Naila and I did not see each other much. Our externship had begun and took up most of our time. Although the Maternité and the St. George weren't too far away, only a few minutes drive, our schedules rarely coincided. We were living in two different worlds.

We agreed to meet one day at a sidewalk café in Hamra at five in the afternoon. I ordered lemonade and observed the flow of a seemingly carefree crowd of passersby. There wasn't a vacant table around me and I realized it had been ages since I had come to this bustling area.

My world had narrowed down considerably and I looked forward to the fall, to my next classes and to seeing familiar faces again. Determined to become a gynecologist, I was learning a lot and enjoying my job at the Maternité. My responsibilities had increased and I had more opportunities to see Sami on a daily basis. His promotion did not change his attitude towards the students and our relationship took its course pretty much as before, except that now I felt a certain distrust towards him.

Every time he smiled at me Fatma's words would come to my mind, and I'd see her pencil moving again. Even though she must have only read my mind, my initial impression of Sami was strengthened. I had no intention of getting involved for the time being anyway.

Fatma's telepathy had a much stronger effect on Naila. A few weeks ago, one of my former patients was being treated at the St. George for acute hepatitis. After visiting her, I passed by the emergency ward hoping to see Naila. Her training required an entire month in the emergency ward, a nerve-racking experience I had to go through last year. Naila was at the front desk giving instructions to a male nurse much taller than her and who was as attentive to her words as to the gestures she was making with a black pen.

When she saw me, she held on to my hand as if afraid I'd leave and told the nurse, "I'll be in the cafeteria for just a few minutes. Call me as soon as the patient regains consciousness."

"How are things with you?" I asked as we crossed sliding doors.

"We have to talk. Do you have time?"

"I have to be back to the Maternité in half an hour," I said looking at my watch.

The cafeteria was empty. Naila had deep circles around the eyes. It reminded me of last year. The sleepless nights. I often had that haggard look myself. "Here," Naila said, after we sat, coffee cups in hand at a corner table. She had pulled a small brown leather pouch from under her shirt.

"The talisman?" I examined it more closely. The square pouch was tightly sealed with tiny black stitches and tied to a long black cord she wore around her neck.

"Fatma told me to wear it all the time," she said, her lips faking a smile.

I said nothing, but something in her eyes worried me.

"Tania, it's either the talisman or this job, but I'm not getting any sleep lately. I'm having nightmares every time I get a chance to sleep."

"You look awful," I said.

"Do you know I don't dare approach the communion table anymore?"

I did not know what to say. I listened attentively as she described the heavily burned patients who had been admitted the previous day and how she had just administered a painkiller to a factory worker who lost three toes loading a refrigerator. When I left I promised I'd call. I could see she was having a rough time but I could not help hoping it would be good for her to be that busy; it would keep her mind off Khalil—except that she kept talking about the talisman.

It seemed the talisman was complicating everything. What was the matter with Naila? I reflected as I was sipping my last drop of lemonade. I was trying to keep my eyes off a tempting chocolate éclair on the pastry tray nearby when Naila sat in front of me. "Sorry I'm late. I had to give my sister a lift, and you know how the traffic is at this hour."

"Let's order some coffee," I said, staring at the dark-haired waiter standing next to us, his back arched like a flamenco dancer. "Or would you rather have something cold first?"

"Coffee is fine. And a glass of ice water," she said running her fingers through her long blond hair, lifting it away from the nape of her neck. She had sounded desperate last night over the phone. She was having more and more terrifying nightmares that she thought were caused by the talisman. When I told her to get rid of it, she said that she did not dare, because it had acquired supernatural powers.

"Tania, can you believe I hear my heartbeat now? I feel my mind is a cavern in which each heartbeat resounds like a gong. It's horrible. I can't help feeling that there is more in that vulgar pouch than just leather, especially when I think of all those stories. The worst part is that I'm so conscious of wearing it! I'm afraid my patients will notice it, or that it will harm them in some way. It's absurd!"

"The only way for you to find peace again is to get rid of the talisman. Why not return to Fatma? Give it back."

"I can't face going back to that house again," she said with an intense look. "I have nightmares that I'm trapped, buried in a giant sepia seashell, in the midst of a raging wind and sandstorm. Besides, it would be like admitting that I don't trust her. I don't want to go back."

"I think you can destroy it by fire or water."

"I have been reading quite a bit lately without finding an answer. Then, I remembered my mother saying that after our maid Aida had died, she had found all sorts of junk under her mattress. Aida had hidden a piece of my mother's satin nightgown in an amulet with strange inscriptions. My mother was told to soak it in a tin full of water for twenty four hours," she said, her eyes disappearing again into her perpetual smile. "The old witch must have hated my mother!"

"Did it work?"

"According to my mother, the so-called allergies that she'd been suffering from for years suddenly disappeared. She is totally convinced of it."

"Do the same thing, then. Here is your answer."

"I'm afraid to do it," she said. "Don't you see, there's no proof there was a curse on my mother. Maybe what she was trying to destroy by water wasn't even a talisman."

"Why not try water first? Then let it dry. And then destroy it by fire. That should take care of it," I said, proud of my inventiveness.

"Please, Tania, I'm not in the mood. You don't realize how serious this matter is. As I was asking people around me, Samia Tawa's maid, who knows a lot about these matters, told me the most horrible things."

"What horrible things? More tales and superstitions," I said raising my eyes towards the sky pretending I wasn't dying of curiosity.

"Samia's maid said that she knew a woman from her village who threw away a talisman in the woods. What happened to that woman was terrible, Tania. As the insects and ants gnawed the talisman, the woman suffered indescribable pains that only ended with the last bit of talisman and her own death. See how human lives can be controlled by formulas and magic?"

"I never thought you'd believe all of that."

"I don't know what to think anymore and I need to concentrate on my work. I can't afford to spend more energy on this matter. I really don't care if there is a curse or not. How could the talisman bring Khalil back to me? I feel for some inexplicable reason like a lost person following her own footsteps over and over again. What if such powers exist, and Khalil is to come back to me on account of the talisman? I don't want a love based on witchcraft."

Naila sounded disturbed. I had nothing to suggest. If she truly believed that all these monstrosities could happen on account of the talisman, then she'd make them happen, somehow. It fit her personality to be so driven. She never let go. I thought of the obsessive fear I had developed as a child after I saw my first vampire movie. I knew vampires feared crosses. At night, at the least suspicious noise, I would hold on tightly to the golden cross I wore on a chain around my neck.

"I have an idea," I said, surfacing from my cloud. "I don't know what it's worth, but I'm thinking of someone who knows more than most people and who will be willing to help us for nothing."

"Who do you have in mind?" Naila said doubtfully.

"*Père* Martin."

"I'm not sure it's a good idea. He'll make fun of us. I doubt a Jesuit priest would know much about these things."

"I don't think there is a subject that Jesuits ignore," I retorted. "Besides, he is not just any Jesuit priest. He has been Dean of the Faculté Française de Médecine for the past ten years, and he's lived in Lebanon for over thirty years. If someone should know how to undo the talisman, it's him."

"What if he makes fun of us?"

"He won't. I'm positive," I said. "I'm sure he will come up with some answers."

"All right," she said, "but you make the appointment."

* * *

I always experienced a strange feeling every time I returned to the university during summer. All activity stopped from June until October. Only the priests, black silhouettes with absorbed, preoccupied looks, could be seen walking hurriedly at times from one building to another.

In the midst of the deserted courtyards and gardens, the buildings' closed doors and staircases seemed out of place, yearning for the bustle and laughter of the students, who would normally press themselves against the walls and columns, sit all over the steps, or walk together in clusters or in pairs. This time, as Naila and I walked towards the Dean's office, I noticed how well the Jesuits kept their premises; the plants and flowerbeds, the alleyways, everything conveying an impression of stillness, as if time were suspended.

Père Martin welcomed us jovially at the door, waved his hands towards the cushioned sofas facing his desk. He had seemed extremely pleased to hear from me and agreed to see us right away. I decided to let Naila do all the talking. She definitely needed no encouragement. I noticed that the talisman had achieved one thing: she had practically stopped talking about Khalil during these past weeks. She had been reading and reading about telepathy, psychics and, of course everything she could find about talismans. Such books were scattered everywhere in her room and in her car.

Père Martin listened to her attentively. I always thought that he had a sweet and noble face. He taught us toxicology. When he lectured, he waved his elongated hands ahead of him as if conducting a march against poisons and toxins. I heard that he spent most of his time researching in an underground lab somewhere in one of the university buildings.

Being an eminence in the scientific world did not make him lose his sense of humor. He always managed to make us laugh in class, even when he evoked the imminent threat of acute or chronic poisoning. "We are surrounded by poisons in our daily lives," he'd say. "Think of the amount of lead present in the butter you consume every day, for instance." I had reached a point where I feared and questioned everything I ate or breathed.

"I understand your dilemma, Naila," he said, rubbing his chin. "You have put yourself in a delicate position. Don't worry. Give me the talisman."

"But, *mon Père*, do you believe all these stories? What is the position of the church towards these powers? And, is there a logical, scientific explanation for all of this?"

"Hum. . . . My dear Naila. Many questions. Difficult answers. The church, as a rule, advises you to stay away from people who pretend to have commerce with the devil. Of course a lot of this, and I speculate, is pure superstition, mere charlatanism." The ebb and flow of his hands intensified as he tried to make his point. "Some of it is, undoubtedly, the result of cultural inheritance, distortion of old beliefs and traditions. Our civilization is still sorting out the sequels of our ancestral paganism. As for science, my dear children, it hasn't said its last word yet. Many unexplained phenomena might, and again, may not be resolved and analyzed scientifically. Especially all manifestations and phenomena grouped under the terminology of the occult. As far as you are concerned, you may go in peace. Stop worrying. Have faith in our Lord Jesus Christ and go on with your lives. A brilliant future awaits you in the medical profession, eh? Do come back to see me. It is always a pleasure, a real pleasure!"

"And the talisman?" asked Naila shyly.

"Oh, yes. Do you have it with you? Fine. I'll take it."

"And how will you destroy it, *Père*?" she insisted.

"Don't worry. I'll dispose of it adequately. You may go in peace."

He conducted us out another door that led to the garden. We began to walk in the back garden behind the library where the Jesuits kept their tropical botanical specimens, and their greenhouse. We both remained silent for a while, enjoying the fact that we had the whole garden to ourselves. We walked by a stonewall adjacent to the library, concealed by crisp garnet-colored bougainvilleas. One could almost forget that, on the other side, the same wall was stacked with bookshelves.

It was cool among all this green under the shade of the intertwined branches of tall rubber and palm trees. I loved walking over the gravel paths. We stopped by a deep, octagonal fountain full of burnt orange fish. We did not come here to take a tour of the garden, I thought. It was a waste of time, after all.

"It did not help much," I said, leaning on the edge of the mosaic border.

"I don't know," Naila said. "I am not sure I expected much of that visit anyway."

I stared at her with surprise.

"After I agreed to come here, I had time to think," she said. "I felt as if a weight was lifted from my shoulders. It was a way of postponing my worries about the talisman. I was already under so much pressure lately. You wouldn't believe the number of patients we've had these past weeks!"

"I think I have an idea," I said. "But what about Fatma's magic? Don't you believe in miracles anymore?"

"I don't know what I believe," she said, smiling. "Sometimes saving a patient seems miraculous. But then it happens so arbitrarily—despite your will or hope. Maybe miracles are just illusions. Khalil loved me. Maybe that was a miracle."

I had nothing to add. I looked sideways at the sun's reflections over the water surface, shaping and reshaping the shadows cast by the leaves above. I thought of Mounir, of the day he came to say good-bye on his way to the airport, his blue eyes full of false tears. Naila and I were not so different after all.

"What do you think he'll do with the talisman?" I suddenly asked.

"Who knows," she said with a half-smile. "He said he'd dispose of it. That could mean almost anything. He may discard it, or forget it in one of his desk drawers."

"He may go to the chapel, asperse it with blessed water— say a few prayers," I said without much conviction. "I hate to say this," I added, "but I wonder if Jesuits, after their intensive studies, still keep their faith intact?"

She ignored my comment and said, "He could take it to the lab, incinerate it or burn it with acid."

"He could," I said, trying to picture the tall black silhouette in the lab, his gray eyes watching the amulet decompose, turn to cinders, his two fingers raised in the sign of the cross, moving in synchronicity with the murmur of litanies.

"I guess we'll never know," I added.

"I guess not. There are many things we don't understand, but I don't think a curse was part of them. I really don't think they played a role between Khalil and me." She paused and said, "Look at these yellow hibiscus. Last year I only noticed pink and red ones."

"I love these flowers. Especially the ones near the fountain," I said, looking at a fat fish come to the surface, attracted by a dragonfly. "I used to enjoy studying here. It's beautiful."

"I did too." She picked up a few grains of gravel in her hand and threw one into the water. The fish disappeared beneath the ripples.

"Did I ever tell you that Khalil and I used to meet in the greenhouse?" she added with a smile as she threw another grain in the font.

"In the greenhouse? That must have been a while ago. It's been years since students were allowed there," I said without mentioning that there was not a corner in the university Mounir and I had not explored.

"The priests are getting tougher every year, huh?" she said. "Tania. You know something?"

"What?"

"I have this strange feeling that it was not me who went to that sepia house. If I hadn't been with you, I'd think I had dreamed of entering a huge, abandoned seashell."

I liked the idea of the two of us trying to reach the remotest point of a convoluted shell—without ever finding it.

"You have been dreaming a lot, lately," I said. "So, you're not sorry we came here?"

"No. I'm glad. Everything looks so peaceful here," she replied. "I see the construction next to the library is finished.

They have expanded the building quite nicely."

"At the expense of the music room. We had such good times in the music room!" I said, watching her throw her last grain of gravel. I imagined they were minuscule shells sinking silently beneath the orange scales wriggling throughout the murky waters.

PERSPECTIVES

On my way back from the hospital, I enjoyed the solitude of the empty apartment. My son Fady was spending the weekend in Jounieh at the Rimal Resort with my brother Joe, who had a chalet overlooking the beach where his family spent most of their weekends. I wasn't sleepy anymore. On the contrary, I felt alert as if I'd slept through the night. Despite the early hour, I poured myself a glass of Armagnac and sat on the leather recliner, oblivious of opening the shades, enjoying the semi-obscurity. I was totally free now and not eager for the day to begin: I needed this time alone. After seven years, Nicole and I just had our second child, but these years weighed on me as if twenty interminable ones had elapsed.

* * *

I remembered Fady's birth, our first years together. When did Nicole and I grow apart? At first, I attributed her change to a difficult pregnancy. Her back hurt constantly and she'd lie in bed or lounge on a couch all day long, reading or watching TV. Where was the energetic young girl, always eager to go out, always ready to have friends over? I gradually took charge of all the chores, thinking it was just temporary, hoping things would get better. With time, I resented coming home early because Nicole would always welcome me with comments like, "Ah, Paul! At last! I bet you forgot the bread again!" or as we'd put the groceries away, she would burst, "What's in your mind? You bought the most expensive cheeses! Don't you check prices?"

Later, when my paintings weren't selling, she didn't miss one opportunity to remind me, "You must switch to a more remu-nerative work, something more . . . commercial! That's the only way to get ahead." It's true that my pay at the Art Institute took care of only our basic needs. I'd spend hours in my studio, staring at half-painted canvasses. I'd sketch some ideas, then put them away, discouraged. The only place where I could concentrate was a loft at my parents' summerhouse, twenty minutes from Beirut in the heart of Broumana, which became my studio. Situated above the garage, in the midst of trees, with windows on all sides, it offered a striking view of the pinewoods and the sea. From there, I enjoyed the changes of seasons as if I were living in the wilderness. I loved this place. It had a private en-trance and I could get in and out without even being noticed. My parents used the house mainly during the hot summer months, when the humidity got unbearable in Beirut. Whenever there, they made themselves invisible to allow me maximum privacy.

Nicole was jealous of the time I spent away from home. "You're not much of a father," she'd complain, "you surely got the easy part." She'd constantly enumerate the projects done by her friends' husbands. I kept hearing that our neighbor John was redoing their landscaping and basement, that Lily's husband was a wonderful cook and helped with the laundry. I tried to be more present, especially spending quality time with my son, but my efforts passed unnoticed because Nicole couldn't bear either to see that I wasn't painting enough. I had to renew myself, find a different style: that's how I'll make it in the "high" circles; that's how I'll find the right clientele. She'd always remind me that inspiration was slipping away and that I lacked motivation. Then came that day when I completed an abstract painting using resin over golden leaf. An abstract composition I considered my best work. A touch of genius, I thought, elated at the daring effects I had created on my canvas . . . until she saw it and asked, "Aren't you going to finish it?" She then added: "And that's what you've been working on for so long?"

For a while, I did portraits in oils and pastels, something I had avoided for a long time. I needed to explore different approaches, but kept getting discouraged by each attempt. I tried to project illusions, boldly explore the instantaneous luminosity that transformed a subject into emotions. But this wasn't going to be an easy route. Once, a businessman objected to his daughter's portrait commissioned for her birthday: "Why isn't it as colorful and lively as these other vivid portraits hanging in your studio?" How could I explain that his daughter was dull and unimaginative and that her own colors directed my palette? I refused to alter the painting.

Nicole took it very badly. "Go ahead, throw our source of income out the window," she frowned. "Your son needs a new pair of shoes, and how do you think we'll pay for them? I should never have had a child so young. I'd be at school getting a business degree."

"You can still do it if you want."

"And who will take care of Fady?"

"What about evening classes?"

"Evening classes, huh? And slave all day at home! Everything seems easy when you're not the one doing it. Why aren't you painting anymore, as you used to, Maestro?"

Of course, there was no point arguing how much I had been doing around the house. Tension increased, and my teaching was affected. I spent more and more time away from home, inventing any kind of pretexts. Nicole seemed to be waiting for anything to go wrong so that she'd have an excuse to recite her frustrations like unending litanies.

* * *

That was when Michelle came into the picture. I'll never forget the day I first saw her seated by the window in the *atelier*, a spacious workshop where I also lectured. She wore her auburn hair shoulder length, sunrays cresting its waves with Venetian blond highlights. She was staring at a poster of *Les demoiselles d'Avignon*, biting her pencil in concentration.

"Do you like Picasso?" I asked.

"I'm a great admirer of your work, *Monsieur* Helou," she replied, ignoring my question.

"You may call me Paul. And you are?"

"Michelle Rahme. I'm new here. My parents just moved from Dahr el Souwan. I'll be attending your Art Theory class and the workshops as well."

"Welcome to the Institute," I smiled, directing myself to the other students arriving at that moment. Michelle. There was music in her name. I had never thought of it, but it felt as if these two syllables had the secrecy of muted notes imprisoned in shells, echoing the hushed murmur of distant waves. Yes, I knew I was overreacting, but it felt good to be recognized. It must have been early fall. Jacarandas' branches were heavy with purple clusters, and bougainvilleas climbing over stonewalls sprouted with an explosion of shapes, offering up variegated colors through tall windowpanes. Michelle always placed her easel close to mine and never lost a word I'd say, making sure to take notes. I remember my repeated glances at the half-open door when she was late. She missed only one day. I strove to incorporate into my lecture the infinite palette displayed beneath the transparent glass, beneath her vacant seat. The students seemed distracted, detached, or was it me? My mind wandered; I was unable to focus on my lesson plan.

The thought of seeing her for as long as the academic year comforted me. The very first thing I'd do upon entering the *atelier* was make sure she was there by the window. Inspired, I spent more time at my parents' loft than ever before, developing techniques and ideas that I presented in class. Michelle's sensitivity to shape and color stunned me. With an innate feeling for art, she understood immediately whatever I'd try to explain. I always questioned her hazel eyes before I'd go any further.

"Michelle, please step up and demonstrate after me, will you?"

"I'll try."

She became my assistant. Quietly, she helped the others with pencil, brush and a minimum of words. She could have passed unnoticed if it weren't for the energy that sparked from her eyes when she talked about art, and her hair, whenever a source of light fell upon it.

She remained reserved until the weeks preceding her departure for Paris, where she had been accepted as an assistant for a young Lebanese artist, Joseph Awad. She came early to class one morning as I was arranging pottery and clay around a draped crimson velours fabric.

"I have a place to stay. My friend Monique, the sculptor, you know, offered to share her flat. She's the one who arranged everything with Awad." She was elated: "And I hope to study Beaux Arts at the Sorbonne. Wouldn't it be marvelous, Paul?"

"Sounds great." That was all I could say, sensing a growing irritation. Why not continue here, after her assistantship was over? I thought to myself. The Lebanese Academy of Fine Arts had produced a great number of talented and world-renowned artists. I had studied there myself. I remembered the day I paced its dark humid lobby, hoping I'd be admitted. Why Paris?

Later that day, we met at La Maison du Café a few blocks from the Institute. We didn't say much as we drank our coffee. She looked at me intently, smiling at times.

"We'll keep in touch," I said.

I could see her struggle to find the right words. "I'll miss you."

"Same."

"You don't understand," she said, uneasily. "It is hard to leave Beirut, you know."

We drove for a while on roads lined with mimosas and palm trees; then we found ourselves surrounded with delicate umbrella pines, their tall parallel trunks steeped in oblique luminous rays, until we reached rocky mountains covered with purple thistle and yellow and blue wildflowers as far as the eye could see. I did most of the talking, telling her about my life with Nicole, how often I had thought of going far away.

I stressed my regained enthusiasm, my projects. I wished I could tell her she was the reason for the energy with which I'd climb the stairs leading to the workshops, to the light shining in her auburn curls bent over a canvas. I couldn't confess I'd look at her sideways, thinking of the many times I had an urge to paint her in class, forget the others in order to capture her hair's brilliance. Between the shadows of passing clouds, delicate hues brightened the vegetation, making it glitter. We weren't far from Broumana and my parents' house. Images of the two of us together were constantly on my mind as we spoke. Time after time, I was about to suggest we'd go there for a while. I'd rehearsed it in my mind; we sort of had a parallel conversation, one real, the other invisible. We'd have some wine, beer, or coffee, I'd show her my paintings, my sketches, the view, she'd get to know my private space . . . I couldn't wait to take her in my arms. I kept silent.

"I envy your freedom," I said, thinking aloud.

"I had to leave. I couldn't bear it anymore . . ." Her voice was monochord, as if she had rehearsed the lines, over and over. I had nothing to say, nothing to offer. Yet she had become part of my life. How could I tell what she had come to mean to me?

She looked at me, expecting me to hold her hand, to kiss her. I almost stopped the car by the side of the road, but instead turned back, beginning the descent towards the city. As it often happens in early spring, on late afternoons, the heavy sky lightened with a fake promise of a new dawn. I drove silently, eyes fixed on the road, indifferent to the unexpected changes around me.

The day before she left, we talked on the phone three, maybe four times. I was in my studio, trying to paint, procrastinating. I'd jump every time the phone rang.

"I'll write," she promised.

"So will I."

When she left, I felt relieved at first. It was only in the evening, right after dinner that I had a sense of numbness in my face, my lips twisting uncontrollably towards my left eye, distorting my vision. It was as if half of me lived passively in the real, concrete world and the other half entered a blurred, phantasmagoric universe, seen through rippled surfaces. A couple of aspirins took care of these symptoms.

These episodes struck me again, for brief periods of time. I enjoyed these melting images, wishing they would last long enough to be reproduced on a canvas. I'd concentrate, try to remember the vision of people cut in half, one half floating on a quiet pond, the other wrinkled under troubled waters. I thought of Dali's limp watches and wondered whether he suffered from migraines. I feared I had become transparent and was witnessing what was going on within my own self, facing the distorted picture I surely offered to others.

She wrote regularly at first. Her letters were brief, her handwriting irregular. I'd run my fingertips over the words, over her name at the bottom of the page, as on a Braille musical score. Around Christmas, I sent her a long letter in a manila envelope, including a sketch of a still life, with an unusual, slanted perspective; the only letter I ever sent. With time, her letters became infrequent.

Did Nicole ever notice any change in me? She was so accustomed to my ups and downs and moodiness. She was also so wrapped up in herself that as long as her needs were met, nothing mattered. I stopped painting for months, and my own bitterness surpassed Nicole's. Never had the tension been greater between us. It was as if electric static were always in the air. I couldn't remember what had brought us together in the first place. I wasn't even seeing her shiny, silky black hair that had once attracted me so much nor her delicately arched eyebrows that she used to raise playfully when we first dated. Now, Nicole and I would sit for hours in the family room by the fireplace, reading, watching TV, without exchanging a word unless it concerned Fady, who had turned five and was excited about beginning soccer practice. I even ignored her compulsive flipping of channels, especially during commercials. I'd open a book, read or work on my lectures, indifferent to what was going on around me.

"What's with you?" she said once, irritated. "It's the third time I've asked you if you were ready to eat!"

"You and Fady go ahead. I'll help myself later."

"Why can't we live normally like everyone else?"

"What's on your mind?"

"Think of us! Of your son . . . of me, for a change. You're always elsewhere."

And she was right. The only reality for me was the one I constantly fabricated around Michelle's image, conjured up through imaginary dialogues. I'd feel her by my side whenever visiting a gallery, admiring a painting or listening to music. She would have loved these brushstrokes or that unusual use of pigments, I was certain of it. Michelle's departure coincided with a major shift in my career. I became involved with local artists who organized cultural exhibits throughout Europe, planning my trips around my teaching schedule. These brief trips—a couple of days, three at the most—enabled me to get away from home, from the perpetual acting that had become my lot, maintaining a wavering status quo.

My bouts of migraine started again, the sharp pain increasing steadily. My head ached almost constantly, and I had to resort to stronger drugs than aspirin. I thought migraines were associated with women, but discovered they could be a major chronic ailment. Some of my friends started telling me how they had dealt with them, giving me all sorts of contradictory therapies that didn't help a bit. All I wanted was to stay away from the network of relations that one can't avoid in our country, beginning with close relatives and extended family. We were constantly invited, and we had to reciprocate sooner or later. Nicole had begun to take pleasure again in socializing, although it barely changed her attitude. Her newfound frivolous trend was weighing on me and I resisted going along. That's when my pilgrimage among neurologists started. My whole vision was fragmented. I felt helpless, worthless . . . my universe was slipping away. I knew there was nothing wrong with me. I simply had to leave Nicole and try to hurt Fady as little as possible. I wished I could go away, live alone in a hut in the Marquises or in an unknown island where all I would do was paint, eat and sleep without seeing anyone. I was ready to go to the other end of the world. Nothing could save our marriage, but I had to regain some peace and strength before I'd face Nicole. That's why I decided to take a short leave with the pretext of meeting other artists organizing an exhibit in Florence. But even from a distance, I kept seeing her split image, half solid, half liquid, half of her accusing, menacing, the other half broken, resigned as if she could read my thoughts. Whenever home, I'd avoid talking, even looking at her. I was waiting for the right time to talk to her. That's when she announced she was pregnant.

FLYING CARPETS

* * *

How could I possibly leave her? I thought of Fady's birth, his tiny bald head, his slanted dark eyes already questioning the world around him. A wave of tenderness submerged me. A boy or a girl, it didn't matter. We were bound to be a family again. From that day on, days succeeded each other, colorless. This time, Nicole had an easier pregnancy, without back pains or unnecessary complaints. She kept busy remodeling the apartment. "It's time to change the wall paper," she said, "I want the baby to come to a perfect home!" "As if the baby had any interest in the decoration," I'd say to myself, never daring to contradict her. Still, I was pleased to see her interest was shifting away from her perpetual criticisms.

I had never immersed myself so much in my work, rising early, sleeping late. I seemed to need fewer hours of sleep. Even the migraines weren't a hindrance anymore. In fact, I considered them an invaluable source of inspiration. I'd endure the pain for as long as I could before taking the medicine and would paint frenetically, consumed by a creative fever. I'd disappear without a word, grateful that Nicole had become more understanding. In such moments, she knew I needed to be alone. I remember the day I imagined a woman's body emerging like a butterfly from a cocoon, her body barely covered with cracked, peeling bark, thin as a veil she was slowly removing. From her head sprouted innumerable arms, branching into more arms, each holding a ripe golden pomegranate. I worked nonstop all night long until the next morning when I fell asleep exhausted on my studio's sofa. I didn't even bother to clean my brushes and palette. When I woke up, I was stunned at that tree woman with no face, a seductive Medusa tempting and arresting, charged with mature fruits ready to burst.

My paintings began to attract attention, and invitations to show in local, regional, and even foreign exhibitions followed. I became obsessed with Phoenician letters. I was intrigued that most of the letters' names were identical to Arabic words: B, *beth*, house . . . G, *gimel* for camel . . . K, *kaph*, palm, yes, and Y, *yodh*, same as hand. The one I particularly liked was O, the perfect shape, called *ayn*, the word for eye! It felt as though I were, in some mysterious way, linked to that remote past. I started to incorporate these symbols in my paintings, modifying them, twisting, elongating them. They became a recurrent theme in my compositions, though not always recognizable, a thread that guided me in the darkness.

My life was finally taking shape, until a week ago, when Nicole announced she changed her mind about calling the baby Leila if it were a girl. "No," she said, determined, "It will be either Mark or Michelle."

"No, no. Not Michelle," I thought! I couldn't bear it. I tried to think of ways to fight it, pretending it reminded me of a boy I hated in elementary school, Michel Lakah. I insisted upon calling her Sulla, Soraya, Elvira, Sofia, Esmeralda, anything less common, more evocative. I insisted so much, Nicole agreed to compromise for the first time in her life: "Fine. We still have time. Let's think of something else, honey."

Then everything happened suddenly. I could barely remember the dream I had the last night just before we went to the hospital. It was so real. I was gasping for air, choking, strangled by hissing serpents. I threw away the smothering blanket, eyes wide-open to the sound of Nicole's alarmed voice, saving me from a certain death: "Hurry, it's time! We have to go to the clinic!" I slipped into my jeans, put a shirt on and helped her with her robe like an automaton.

"Get the suitcase, quick," she said with a faint voice, her face taut with pain as she held her belly.

We took the elevator down to the ramp and got into the car. I adjusted her seat until she reached a comfortable position and then started the car, fumbling for the ignition with shaking hands. I needed coffee. It was two in the morning. I tried to concentrate on the road, careful to avoid any jerky movement of the car, having a hard time keeping my eyes open. It was drizzling. Pearly drops gathered into faint, solitary lines and the wet asphalt of deserted avenues and sidewalks shone beneath hazy streetlights. I felt as if we were sailing over dark waters under the moonlight.

We were nearing Dr. Sawaya's clinic in Achrafieh. Nicole was breathing rhythmically. The raindrops hit harder, echoing the wipers' nervous whistle. Fully awake, my throat dry, I pulled up to the emergency lighted entrance and stopped carefully. As I helped Nicole out of the car, a young man in a windbreaker rushed towards us holding an outstretched black umbrella, and asked for the car keys. In the waiting room, Nicole sat, moaning, legs apart, on an uncomfortable vinyl chair while I filled out the admission form. Two male nurses entered with a stretcher and took her away. I tried to follow them but the receptionist stopped me: "One moment, Sir. Please wait until the doctor allows you inside."

What about Fady? I thought in a flash, What if he wakes up and doesn't find us home? Then I remembered he was staying at his uncle's beach house with his cousins. I stared at the old woman seated across from me. She seemed distant. I rubbed my eyes, and looked around me. The empty chairs seemed to sway. A nurse walked in after an indefinite lapse of time and looked at the old woman then at me with inquisitive eyes.

"How is my wife? Can I see her, now? "

"Congratulations!" she said, smiling. "You have a beautiful baby girl. It was an easy delivery. Your wife's fine. She's expecting you."

I followed the white shape through narrow corridors framed by half-open doors. We entered a spacious room with drapes closely drawn, separating several beds. Nicole was in the first bed, by the entrance, reclined over pillows: an older nurse sat by her side, holding a baby with jet black hair, blue eyes and perfectly defined features.

"You can only stay a minute," said the nurse. "Your wife must rest now."

"Her mouth is perfect," I said, kissing Nicole on the cheek, unable to turn my eyes away from the baby. Nicole seemed tired but beamed with joy despite the circles around her half-closed gray eyes.

"Yes, she is lovely," she said with a sleepy voice, "and so tiny. She has your eyes, Paul. Here, hold her."

I was surprised at the baby's weightlessness. So much life in store in that miniature.

"Let's call her Michelle, honey," I said.

She rolled onto her side and closed her eyes. I needed to go home and sleep. Sleep, that's all I could think of, all that really mattered.

THEY WON'T MISS ME THIS AFTERNOON

They won't miss me this afternoon. I left the house when Nadia opened the door to Mrs. Khoury, the old neighbor.

"Listen, Nadia, I've just heard that more roads are blocked," Mrs. Khoury said. "We may have to go without fresh vegetables and fruits again."

"Come in," said Nadia. "Let's have coffee and talk. I need a break before the kids return from school."

I usually enjoy Mrs. Khoury's gossip. But today, I've decided to take a walk. I'll be back before dinnertime. No one will even notice my absence.

Nadia has been busy all day. It is our turn to have the bridge group over this evening. She set small tables in the living room, covered them with a green felt tablecloth. I remember the long evenings she spent cutting hearts, diamonds, clubs and spades in red and black felt. Then, she festooned them meticulously. It took her months to complete the bridge mats. She delicately arranged the patterns around the border and secured them with invisible stitches, sometimes by candlelight. Electric power failures were part of life then. Nadia once said, "I have become a nocturnal animal. I see in the dark like a cat."

She placed ashtrays, pencils and notebooks on the tables. Satisfied, she set forth to the kitchen. For a couple of hours, I watched her make a Black Forest cake. She carefully sliced the cake, pursing her lips in concentration, filled it with whipped cream and Maraschino cherries. Later, she covered the frosting with chocolate shavings, bark and mini-logs. Whipped cream is my weakness. I always get to lick the bowl.

I had forgotten the street smells. A renewed, forgotten life penetrates my senses. Jasmine hedges and tamarind mix a strong cocktail faintly tainted at times by cars' exhausts. I love the emanations coming from restaurants' cooking. There are quite a few around here. I think I smell fried fish. Today must be Friday then, because I heard Nadia ordering sole fillets, over the phone, for tonight's dinner. At this very moment, Nadia is probably asking Mrs. Khoury to give her recipes for new sauces.

I imagine the two women sitting in the kitchen. The curve of Mrs. Khoury's back brings her face to her waist. She always thrusts her chin forward when walking as if it were an antenna. She loves to be the center of attention. Her stories are punctuated by her chin pointing in different directions, dragging along her round head, around which two long braids are rolled like white ropes. She hushes everything in a low, raucous voice. With this war lasting for more than twelve years, she never lacks dramatic stories to tell.

I don't go out often anymore. I grew out of the habit because of the uninterrupted shelling. Lucky there's a remission now. No fighting, no bombs exploding in months. Things are calming down. I'm getting old. I should get some fresh air now and then. I'm almost an object in the house. When friends visit, I sit comfortably aside on a sofa by the window, lean on a silk pillow. My eyes follow the sun's reflections all over the room. Sometimes, I close my eyes, pretend I'm sleeping, but I remain attentive to every single word they say.

It's fun to walk along the narrow sidewalks. There are fewer sandbags now. Everything seems peaceful. Young boys in uniforms sweep the streets and hold their post in intersections. It's quiet at this hour. Only a few women beat the pavement with the weight of their grocery bags. A new beauty salon has opened next to the L'Éclair's bakery: Coiffure Latifa. I heard Nadia's friends say, "It is always full. Incredible, considering the prices!" I watch women coming in and out the revolving doors. People have learned to live from day to day and enjoy the present moment to its fullest. A tall lady is just coming out, smiling. Maybe convinced that her new hairstyle fits her crescent carved profile.

I continue downhill. The road slopes slightly; I'll worry about it on my way back. I reach a vegetable stand. Vegetables and fruits gorged with sun look the same year after year. A fat woman with red swollen cheeks argues, "A hundred pounds for a kilo of tomatoes! What are you trying to do? Starve us?"

"Go grow your own," says the merchant, menacing. "We're risking our necks crossing the city from one end to another. It's getting more dangerous everyday." His rough stained hands delicately rearrange the symmetry of the tomato heap. He wipes the ones on top with a cotton rag.

"One hundred pounds!" repeats the fat woman. "They only cost a pound before the war."

She leaves without the tomatoes.

Mrs. Khoury's words come to my mind. We could go through another difficult period. It wouldn't be the first time we'd live on rations. Luckily, we never lacked food so far. We'd go to our summerhouse in the mountain. There, in Reyfoun, we have a beautiful orchard: peaches, apples, pears, and plums. It is breathtaking in spring. By the front of the house, vegetables grow almost without care. Giant mountain tomatoes, parsley, onions, zucchinis. . . . A fellow from the area looks after it in our absence.

Half the summer was spent canning. The kitchen was converted into a real lab. All operations were timed. Vegetables and fruits were blanched or pasteurized. Nadia was proud of her jars. We'd bring them all down at the end of the summer to Beirut in several trips. They were everywhere, on the shelves, over the counters, inside and on top of the cabinets.

It sprinkles a little. I walk faster to get under the nearby arcades. Many businesses are relocated in East Beirut now. Some people are rebuilding their store for the third time. The East side has grown to be quite self-sufficient, at least for everyday needs. Women practically never go to West Beirut, unlike men, who have to go back and forth for business. But it is much safer, now.

I cross the next set of barricades. So many things have changed everywhere, nevertheless, I know my way home. Here and there, broken pipes pop out under the opened concrete, spitting water like a spring over the asphalt. It's surprising to see clear water coming out of the entrails of the earth.

A girl washes laundry in a plastic bucket right in the middle of the sidewalk. She throws the gray sudsy water on the side, rinses and wrings strongly. I've heard of refugees from Tyre and Sidon who take shelter in empty houses. They come with their bundles, sometimes a goat or a pair of chickens. I hear a long moan. No, it's a song. Children's voices intone a funeral hymn. Some kids walk in line like in a procession. They carry on their shoulders a couple of nailed planks on which graffiti read: "God forgive" and "Rest in peace." I must have walked a long time. I'm tired and dread the long way back. The kids stare at me with empty eyes. They've just noticed me. They put their planks aside, approach me carefully, pointing their long sticks like machine guns.

"Call Mohsen," orders the oldest, "Go!"

Nadia's friends used to smile at me, "Your cat's fur is as shiny and soft as black mink. It's very well taken care of." Her husband once complained, "You're crazy! If anyone knew you fed that cat chicken livers when people are starving. . . ."

"I couldn't get near those people if I wanted to," she replied. "I have no way of helping them. You know it. Besides, the cat only eats leftovers. It doesn't cost us anything."

"Look! He is a real big one!" The boys are getting really excited. I can tell they aren't after my fur.

"Mohsen! Over there, shoot, shoot, hurry! Don't let him get away!"

III

ANEMONE'S FINGERS

Lina waited patiently for the Butterfly fish to come out from one of his favorite hiding places. She spent hours daily at the neighbor's apartment, scrutinizing the coral branches, shells and anemones, from which her silver fish could emerge unexpectedly. She never guessed what direction he would come from. It wasn't really her fish, but it was the one she had selected as the most beautiful of all of Sonia's tropical fish. In addition, the little girl thought he needed special care and was lonely. She had told Sonia: "There is only one of his kind in the whole aquarium."

When Sonia noticed Lina's fascination for this marine world, she gave her permission to feed her precious fish. Gradually, Lina discovered that "her" fish was shy. Unlike the rest of the fish that would instantly gather at the surface, attracted by the slightest ripple, he'd take his time, and glide minutes later, in the now quieted aquarium. For this reason, Lina kept his share in her left palm and would only cast the dried flakes when he finally appeared.

The fern-like green algae wavered in the silent aquarium along with the multi-fingered anemones as if an undercurrent, caused by the fish's gentle traffic, had blown a tenuous underwater breeze.

The Fan Worms' feathery tentacles were imperceptibly swaying, and the aquarium was returning to its quasi-static state, when the triangular silver and orange striped fish suddenly leafed his way through the purple anemones. Lina wondered what it would feel like to lightly touch the fluorescent pink tip of the white anemone's slender fingers. They looked like giant chrysanthemums breathing rhythmically in all directions, a multitude of pink eyes thrust in unison.

"Here he is, Sonia. Come quickly," the little girl said, brushing her palms over the surface. "Why don't you have another fish like him?"

"I don't know. They are hard to find, I guess," replied Sonia, as she watched the transparent blue silver fins fringing the black spot mimicking the rimmed eye on a flaming peacock's feather. "But we will get another one eventually. Now, do you want to help me with the wool or does your mother expect you home? How does she feel today?" added Sonia.

"She says she's fine. But that's what she always says. She has to deliver a dress tonight to Mrs. Haddad and she probably won't need me right away. I can stay for a while."

Sonia had been working on a baby's layette for the past ten years with the passion of an expectant mother. She had not given up hope of getting pregnant and knitted and crocheted tirelessly, often undoing a whole scarf or an entire outfit whenever she made the slightest mistake. Lina often helped her roll the wool in tight balls and wrap the finished clothes in scented silk paper. Then Sonia would stack them in the nursery drawers and cupboards, careful to add mothballs in every corner. Sonia and her husband Tony had decorated the nursery in neutral shades, ochre and earth tones. The first years they only had a crib, but they soon decided to add a bed, large enough to accommodate their unborn child until adolescence.

And so, little by little, the couple had become accustomed to the presence of the unborn child as if a baby were actually living there and growing. They constantly shopped and made provisions for the child's needs. As Sonia decided to take up sewing for her progeny, she needed the help of a seamstress. That's how she first met Lina's mother, Elham, who lived in an apartment on the same floor at the opposite side of the building.

The two women became friends and Sonia frequently visited the seamstress who welcomed her company. Elham seldom talked about herself and avoided mentioning her husband, Nagi, whom Lina had never known. When the little girl was only one year old, he took a trip to Brazil to visit relatives his father had grown up with, and who had decided to emigrate. After a few letters saying how much he missed the family, Nagi stopped writing and no one had heard of him since.

Left on her own, Elham worked at a renowned tailor's shop, Majeed Boustany, who relied heavily upon her until her health deteriorated. A couple of years ago, she discovered she had a malignant tumor. Since then, Elham had to work from home. She hardly left the apartment except for the chemotherapy sessions, and spent her days bent over the sewing machine giving shape to her clients' multicolored fabrics. Lina had grown accustomed to her mother's tired looks, and the deep circles around the eyes that left her expressionless. The long white shirt she always wore while working was constellated with silver pins and needles. Elham's fingers moved with dexterity, her thumb and forefinger sticking and pinning the needle so quickly it seemed as though the fabric were ethereal. Lina watched her mother's fingers—the smaller ones always covered with metal thimbles—run over the fabric, smoothing it at times, or guiding it firmly with both hands under the mechanical ticking of the Singer's needle.

The little girl helped her mother as much as a ten-year-old could. Not only did she do the errands but she also learned to fix simple meals. "Lina, could you take this package to the fifth floor," her mother would say. Or, "Lina, please find my needle, I have dropped it on the floor somewhere." Or "Bring me a cup of tea." And "Lina this," and "Lina that." One of her responsibilities was to water the luxuriant ferns that Elham couldn't resist buying and were crowding the small apartment. "They bring me a breath of fresh air," she'd say. Lina found it natural to look after her mother, reminding her to take her pills and assisting her at night when she felt sick.

She was a quiet and silent child who collected leftover pieces of colorful fabric, ribbons, and silver and gold trimmings. She had several cardboard boxes full of damask squares, velvet triangles, brocade and silk stripes. One day, while Sonia, flanked by her inseparable needlework, was visiting with Elham, she discovered the girl's treasure and offered to give her samples of her unused yarn and wool. From that day on, Sonia found a devoted helper in Lina as well as a good listener, someone who would be interested in her ongoing projects. "What do you think of that afghan, Lina? Isn't it darling?" she'd say, showing her a picture in a baby's magazine, or "Look at this white bedspread sprinkled with daisies! See, their center is made of fluffy pompons. They're easy to do, I'll show you."

When Sonia and Tony decided to have an aquarium, Lina couldn't let a day pass without stopping by. During the winter, she came after school to visit and admire the couple's newest acquisitions. Tony was particularly proud of the aquarium. He felt it would distract Sonia from her obsessive knitting and crocheting. They spent time visiting aquariums, delighted at discovering new striking species, along with decorative seashells and companion plants indispensable to the fish's well-being. They found an incentive to go out, and lingered hours in bookstores and libraries reading about exotic fish behavior and special care.

After a period of excitement that lasted a few months, the aquarium reached its final state: it was the most beautiful aquarium Sonia and Tony could dream of. They both enjoyed contemplating the iridescent fish appear and disappear amid the variegated green algae, beneath the coral growths, then retreat within the winding shells' innermost recesses. Watching the fish became an important part of their daily routine, especially during the evenings, when the built-in lights enhanced their glowing reflections. The couple divided their responsibilities: Tony took care of the tank's cleanliness and temperature, and Sonia was in charge of the food.

But very quickly, Sonia returned to her long silver needles, and her balls of wool reappeared again on the living room's sofa. She was pleased to see Lina take over feeding the fish. It was the little girl's favorite pastime, and the child's joy was a good excuse for Sonia to dedicate herself fully to her passion: producing more and more layette for her child-to-be. Sonia suddenly realized that she would soon need a new commode in which to store her work, but she thought, "Soon the child will come and outgrow the clothes. There will be enough room then."

One day, Sonia was knitting a blue afghan while she was having coffee at the seamstress'. The women's shiny needles kept busy as Sonia talked and Elham listened, listened and never answered. It seemed that the circles around her eyes were getting larger and purple, as if veins were multiplying at the surface of the skin. With great effort, Elham's shears were biting their way through a thick woolen fabric. She interrupted Sonia's continuous chat. "The doctor wants to keep me at the hospital overnight for additional tests. Could Lina spend the night with you?" She should not worry, Sonia said. The little girl would sleep in the nursery. "You know that I have no one," Elham continued in a faint voice. "All you need to worry about is getting better," said Sonia, "What are friends and neighbors for?"

That night, Lina waited a long time by the aquarium for her fish to show up before she could go to sleep. Some fish hid behind the brown and green algae while some nestled under the coral sand. At times, only a couple of Tangs or Angelfish were visible, moving freely in the empty tank, taking over the whole aquarium. She wished she could see beyond the coral reefs, within their crevices and galleries. She imagined a complex world in which words were replaced by the vibrations of ethereal fins. She wondered if the fish knew it was time to go to sleep, if they were in any way connected to humans' daily cycle. Unable to answer these questions, she followed Sonia to the nursery. "See," said Sonia, "You will have the nursery all to yourself. Sleep well. Good night."

Lina could see every detail in the nursery despite the darkness. She knew the plush animals one by one, and her eyes checked every corner of the shelves and drawers, as though the toys and clothes were phosphorescent. She fell asleep in the middle of a forest of white algae, leaning over pillows of white coral reefs, soft as plush. She saw herself surrounded by a school of translucent Butterfly fish, all replicas of her silver fish, with violet circles around the eyes. They all had an extra eye, a black spot, also circled with bright purple.

Carried away deeper by the current, she wondered what it was like to dive in the soft coral sand, what it was like to be a fish, a silver fish, to go everywhere together, side by side, without ever being able to face each other with both eyes. Condemned to a side-glance, always. She reached out to hold her fish, but she could only wave transparent fins. Fish could never hold each other. Never! She woke up crying, tears all over her face, to find herself in the middle of the night in the white nursery among the plush animals. She wondered if her mother was lonely in a white hospital bed. She wiped her face with the sheet and went back to sleep.

Lina spent the next morning shopping with Sonia. "Mother will be back this afternoon," she said. Elham was always tired when she came back from the hospital and Lina tried to imagine what she could do to welcome her. "I'll clean up my room and also the whole house," she decided. She began with her drawers, and rearranged the toy shelves. "That will make Mom happy," she thought.

Then she sorted out the dresses and skirts scattered all over the tiny living room. "Our house is always so messy in comparison to Sonia's," she thought. But she would surprise her mother, and hang all the finished dresses separately. She knew how. She had seen her mother do it day after day. In the sewing box, Lina placed the silver thimbles and colored bobbins in their compartments. She also removed the scissors and pieces of chalk and markers that were scattered on the table. Then with a magnet in the shape of a horseshoe, she started picking up the shining pins covering the tables, the clothes, littering the carpet. As she gathered the pins from beneath the carpets' shags, the image of her mother pinning the needles all over her shirt and lapel came to her mind. She thought of her mother wearing a dress made out of needles, like scales, of her mother in the hospital, her white body covered with shiny needles, and the circles around her eyes getting bluer and bluer.

When Lina felt that everything was in its right place, she decided to take a bath. She had refused to shower at Sonia's house, but she would get ready now for her mother. She ran a bath and checked the water's temperature. "I wonder what temperature the fish really like," she thought, and worried, "Was Mom kept warm last night?" The child pictured a series of cold metallic hospital beds. She took off her clothes and sank in the bathtub wishing it were a giant aquarium. Lina covered her eyes with her palms, rubbed them strongly as she customarily did when she was alone. The phosphorescent fish appeared once more, in different shades, but coupled now. She sensed the rhythm of their movements as they went back and forth in the aquarium in a mute tango in which the partners would not touch, perfect doubles, mimicking the music's faint echo. The fish disappeared in far away niches when Sonia knocked insistently at the door.

"Lina, hurry up! It's me. Sonia." Lina finished her bath, got dressed and went to Sonia's apartment. "Everything is ready for Mom," she said proudly.

"Your mother called," said Sonia avoiding the child's eyes. "She said that the doctor wants her to spend another day or two at the hospital. Don't worry. You will stay with us. We will go visit her as soon as possible."

The little girl followed Sonia everywhere, like a shadow, silently helping the woman with her chores, listening to her unending flow of words. Sonia had bought new baby fashion magazines and was busy marking the clothes she liked best. She always tried to select styles and colors that would equally fit a girl or a boy, continuously asking for Lina's opinion. But she could not get the child to respond as usual.

Lina's face came to life when it was time to feed the fish. She stared a while at the untroubled aquatic life. She watched the retractile anemone's fingers; they seemed thicker, and softer—caressing like her mother's restless fingers. Tiny bodies nestled in their midst, some only discernible by a touch of color. Lina threw some flakes into the water, and vibrant pieces of scintillating silk and muslin rushed to the surface. The parallel iridescent stripes covering some fish curved into arabesques towards the edges and faded near the fins into spots of luminous shades. She paused a long time before she added the second portion of dried flakes. Her silver fish was there, a flaming feather, deceiving her once more, she thought, unable to figure out where he had been hiding.

When Sonia left Lina that night in the nursery, she bent down and kissed the child good night. Lina stared at the white room, eyes wide open, looking at the nursery as if for the first time. She did not remember what exactly was stacked in the drawers, behind the cupboards. It would take her all night to figure it out again, she thought. The room looked different, unfamiliar, like an impersonal hospital room. Sonia and Tony stayed up late, talking and talking for hours. "I could not tell her," Sonia kept repeating. "I just could not. I will have to talk to her before the social worker comes this week."

Sonia woke up later than usual, more tired than she had felt in a long time. She looked at her face in the bathroom mirror. She had wide circles around her eyes. Sonia imagined Elham, lying alone in the hospital, and never to come back. She went to the nursery to wake Lina up. The child loved to sleep in late in the morning. When Sonia opened the curtains, she found an undone bed, the white sheets contrasting with Lina's blue pajamas. She looked around, kneeled to peak under the bed, checked every corner of the house. There was no sign of Lina, except for her blue pajamas and the clothes she wore the day before, neatly folded on top of the commode.

Sonia ran to the child's apartment with growing anxiety. She chased the images that kept imposing themselves on her mind, and refused to panic: the little girl had to be in her own bed, or in her mother's bed. For some reason, she missed her own home. But there was no sign of Lina anywhere. Unable to think, Sonia called Tony. He decided to go to the police station. "This is the only thing we can do," he said. Sonia spent the day knitting nervously next to the phone, staring at the needles' motion. The needles clicked and clicked with frenzy as in an unending fencing contest. She had lost sense of time. The afghan was growing visibly, covering her knees, reaching her ankles. She kept telling herself that the child ought to be somewhere near, hiding close-by. Had Lina overheard their conversation last night or was she trying to see her mother at the hospital? Lina acted so differently yesterday, Sonia thought, she may have sensed what had really happened, that her mother would never come back this time.

Tony came home late that night. He had stopped again at the police station after leaving work. He noticed the circles around Sonia's eyes, and said reassuring, "They will find her tomorrow. The police officer said it was not uncommon for children to disappear just like that. She may come back on her own, you know." Sonia realized that she had not cooked, nor thought of dinner all day. She had not looked at anything except her needles. She had even forgotten to feed the fish. Sonia subconsciously mimicked the child's behavior, casting the first portion of flakes in the tank. She imagined Lina staring at the fish's peaceful race, the child's eyes wide open, her admiring gaze. Only when Lina watched the aquarium did she ever look so immersed, so genuinely happy. Sonia added the second portion and rubbed her palms gently over the tank as Lina always did to rid her hands of the slightest crumb.

In a flash, a pair of triangular silver striped fish appeared from behind the coral branches, fluttering their flaming orange peacock's tail. They moved in synchronicity, taking their time in the now settled aquarium, like actors glittering under the stage's spotlights. Only the fish could see Sonia's startled expression. She stared at the aquarium, motionless. Even her husband's voice, coming from the bedroom, "They will find her tomorrow," breaking faintly through her mind, could not lift her from her perplexity.

THE FISHERMAN

The boat glided, phantomlike, over the dense waters barely touched by the first rays of dawn. Convinced she wouldn't reach their destination, she hadn't asked where they were headed. Seated in a corner, she watched his rugged hand roll the anchor rope around a pole. His pupils, enlarged in the semi-darkness, gave life to his green, expressionless eyes. He looked through her as if she were transparent. Unable to bear this, she closed her eyes, cradling her belly with her hands, and thought of the metallic gray eyes, which had captivated her youth.

Those gray eyes were the backdrop to so many dreams, taking her through closed doors, beyond the island's infinite horizon. He was called the voice of the sea, the teller of wonders, yet he was no more than an ordinary fisherman selling fish, shells and corals by the village well, weaving stories as he mended his nets. He'd linger there under the sun until it reached its zenith, surrounded by children and idlers who awaited him from the days' early hours. Hidden in the large folds of their pleated pants or wraparound gowns were humble gifts they placed by his nets. No one knew his real name, or where his numerous tales sprang from. He knew of faraway lands where tamed condors obeyed men, helping them hunt, plant seeds and harvest in the mountain tops, of fortresses built by condors in inaccessible peaks touched only by snow.

She remembered how she was always first by the well, eager to be near him, captured by the magic of his words, unfolding colorful worlds. He disclosed what she came to call the gates of truth, transporting her beyond the village walls, beyond the endless boundaries of the sea. Later, during her adolescent years she'd escape her seclusion in the convent, open these gates as she conjured images of the shimmering seaways bursting with iridescent moonfish that constantly followed his boat in deep furrows.

Seated cross-legged, face bent over his nets, he'd carefully examine every tangle, the tightness of every knot while tirelessly retelling what he alone had witnessed, as if addressing an invisible presence. He would turn his head at times, his piercing eyes would stare at the crowd, as though he needed to reassure himself of their attention. He'd describe how fish caught in his net would change color instantaneously, marveling at the greens, turquoises, purples, yellows, turning ashen gray. He'd recall how long it took him to pull the nets so heavy with fish, he almost heard their lament. Separated from the waves, the fish could still smell the ocean in multitudes of suspended salty drops, in seaweeds tasting of freedom, unaware of the irreversible fate possessing them in the shape of an invisible web. They frenetically jumped, tails and fins erect, ensnaring themselves more and more in the woven trap, the false sense of freedom fading in a last tremulous quiver. Later, the deflated net would rest on the deck, scales sliding against glistening scales, sticking together in an amorphous mass. Here and there a nervous spasm, a flicker shaking a transparent fin or silvery tail, they lay, vibrant eyes wide open, mouths fixed in an almost human rictus of despair.

Moved by their irrevocable fate, she loved best the stories in which fish grew wings or those where condors with human features built entire villages in the highest branches of gigantic Thuley trees. The ebb and flow of his stories paralleled his gestures as he flipped the net open in a circular movement to check a tear, then threw it on the ground as he examined every single mesh. He'd hurl it again in the air to punctuate his words, swelling the net with waves, winds, crests and peaks until he'd put it aside, folding it in special creases like bookmarks. At that time, he would silently wrap the gifts of dried fruits, loaves of bread and round cheese in large fig leaves that he placed in a bag of cloth he threw over his back, carry his empty baskets and leave. For a while, all would remain in the same position, still captivated by his enchanted visions. He often used strange words no one understood and after he left, each listener would elaborate a different version of his tales.

Then came that stormy night when the entire village gathered under pouring rain, lightning and hurling winds, awaiting news from the rescue teams. Many did not return, their fragile skiffs and fishing boats caught in the worst tempest they had seen in years. The fisherman was among the casualties, unconscious and severely wounded, his maimed arm hanging as they carried him hurriedly to a nearby shelter. "He's dead," the young girl thought, with sadness. Blood stained his torso and torn shirt. She noticed a bright whiteness around the wound, which brought to her mind the image of a dying albatross she once watched, its white feathers glued with blood.

Mata, her father's companion came to her, and held her tightly, saying with difficulty: "There was nothing I could do. Nothing. I will take care of you, child. I promised him I'd protect you." She couldn't feel anything. She looked at the man without seeing him, wishing it were her father who had returned instead. She wished they had brought him back on a stretcher, wounded and unconscious. She knew she would have healed him. Mata kept staring at her. He was soaked, his face and arms bruised, yet she felt nothing inside.

She was only two when her mother died and had to grow faster than other children, doing chores around the household, taking care of herself during her father's constant absences. As long as she could remember, his closest friend Mata had always been around, sharing good and bad times with his fishing partner. But now she was truly alone. She didn't sleep that night, hoping her father hadn't suffered too much, trying very hard to remember him as she had seen him last, handsome and laughing. The following days, the entire village seemed foreign, all were busy in repairs, funerals and mourning. She saw so much pain, despair or resignation in people's faces that she decided to stay home. When Mata made arrangements for her to study in a convent in the mountains, she was relieved to distance herself from all that sorrow.

Her years at Le Refuge were happy ones. Mata came to visit occasionally, bringing modest presents to the nuns, mostly fresh catch or orange baskets that they greatly appreciated. She felt fortunate she had someone in the outside world. She missed the sea and talked often of the village life before that tragic night, remembering every detail through the fisherman's stories, unable to separate the two worlds constantly intertwined in her mind. She'd unlatch the gates of truth of his shimmering words and try to reconstruct the visions conjured up by the movements of the fisherman's net and piercing eyes. When the time came to decide if she would become part of the religious community or marry, Mata came more regularly to the convent, conferring at length with the Sisters.

It only seemed natural to her that she would return to the village as Mata's wife. She had no one else, after all, and sensed it would be what her father wished for her. She was glad to smell the sea breeze again and spent long hours walking barefoot along the shore. In charge of prolonged fishing expeditions, Mata was away most of the time, often for months. A solitary child, she did not mind his long absences. She grew vegetables in her backyard and sold them in the village square. The village had grown and no one gathered around the well any longer. She inquired about the fisherman but no one had seen or heard of the storyteller.

She would find out much later, by chance. One day, as she ventured very far, chasing seagulls, she reached the extreme end of the island. She was walking by the lighthouse, when she passed a man with rolled up trousers, seated cross-legged on the beach. He was blowing softly into a spiral seashell, and as he turned slightly at her approach, she recognized his hard metallic eyes. Eager to know what had happened to him, she sat by him on the wet sand. Her heart leapt in her tightened chest, bursting with desire to tell him how well she remembered his stories, and that she thought she would never see him again.

He had not died that night in the storm, he explained, but was left with the use of only one arm and a bad knee. Friends cared for him during his lengthy convalescence. Unfit for sailing, or fishing, unable to dive for corals and seashells, he became the keeper of the lighthouse. Avoiding people and crowds, he rarely went to the village, and then, only at sunset. Gradually, he disappeared from the village's memory and no one recalled he was once known as the voice of the sea.

From that day on, she returned often at the same hour and would encounter him, his shells lined on the sand, meditating, feet licked by the tides' foam. She would ask him questions about inaccessible citadels with domes, spires and minarets, curious to know if the inhabitants of Thuley trees ever descended to earth with ladders or spent a lifetime up there, surrounded at night by the constellations. She wondered how they moved from one house to another and if the condors, or condorlike creatures spoke human language. He patiently answered her questions, uncovering unsuspected aspects of the tales she thought she remembered. He would bring to his ear the pink Conch then the Harp shell and teach her their secret notes. Sometimes, children or passersby would stop and he'd interrupt his sentence, sorting the shells, filling them with golden sand, emptying them slowly until they left.

His company had set aside the clouds of bitterness she had grown accustomed to. Grateful for having recovered her lost affections, she felt unworthy of such happiness. With the innocence of youth, she went to the lighthouse, climbing the stairs in her flowered dress, her long hair scented. Seated halfway in the spiral staircase they shared the provisions she brought in a knotted handkerchief. She came to him as into her own, not thinking twice in unveiling her thoughts and feelings, the way a child shows a hesitant drawing to his parents in exchange for praise or caress. In the lighthouse, they made love night after night in absolute darkness as if suspended in the cool labyrinths of an enormous seashell.

As days went by, her recklessness increased while he often appeared preoccupied. He seemed to have a secret he needed to share, but was reluctant to disclose, even to her. He often sighed, "I wish I could take you away, far away, but it's impossible. I'm no longer the man I was." And he'd say, "Sometimes the memory, if kept alive, is more powerful than life itself. I can protect myself, trust me. It's you I worry about. . . ." "I would do anything, anything he'd ask for, except leave him," she thought, reading his mind. Besides, she had a feeling Mata would find out anyway, no matter what they decided to do.

Whenever Mata was around, she could not hide the fact that she was always tired and sleepy. He surely noticed how her complexion got paler day after day and soon she wouldn't be able to dissimulate the changes in her figure. She could no longer bare the thought of any physical contact with a man she respected as a father. Now, whenever she rubbed his aching back with medicinal oil, her fingers would burn like fire. They would turn red and swell, yet it was the same oil she had often applied on his sore muscles before. "I can't go on, Mata," she'd say, "See, this oil has gone rancid. It's not good anymore." Mata would feel some of the oil between his thumb and forefinger, smell it repeatedly and conclude, "It's all in your head. I see no difference."

It had become harder for her to meet the fisherman in the lighthouse and whenever she'd manage to escape, their love-making had become desperate. He seemed to have a thirst for weaving together the eclectic threads of his various tales, incorporating recurrent images into a harmonious, lustrous fabric as if he was bringing closure to the whole. He talked incessantly about condors, describing their feathers, the elegance of their flight, and their devotion to humans. He told of men and women with condor wings, who had once been condors billions of years ago, but who had reached a quasi-perfect form through perilous trials.

These vivid images accompanied her constantly, appeasing her growing anxiety. Yet, she knew right away that something was wrong that evening, when Mata, upon returning home, asked her to pack all she would need for a long trip. "We'll leave tomorrow before dawn," he said, before he slammed the door and left, ignoring the dinner awaiting him on the table. Something indefinable had changed in him, somehow the fluidity of his green eyes had disappeared. Although a good man, the mariner was known to be violent, never forgiving his men for a mistake. She ran to the door, with only one thought in mind, to run to the lighthouse. But the door was locked. She lay down and stared for hours at the ceiling, helpless, fearing the worst. A few hours later, Mata came home and threw himself on the bed, stone drunk, with his boots and clothes on.

Well before dawn, she was ready and followed him into the boat. Rearranging the bundle of clothes behind her back, she felt her belly, eyes closed, and thought of him, hoping he'd be safe as he always assured he'd be. She sensed he was in no danger, opened her eyes and faced Mata. She knew she had wronged him but how could he ever understand? She didn't understand herself. Startled, she noticed blood on his shirt and her heart pounded uncontrollably. Following her look, he grinned, "I paid him a visit last night. Almost got that louse! Hypocrites! He's wounded all right. Huh. But he managed to escape in that damned tower of his."

Noticing her expression of relief, he added grimly, "But not for long. I nailed a few planks at the door. He won't get away." She closed her eyes again. She dreamed of him flying, chest and neck covered with white down, thought of the bloodstained down she glimpsed on his arm the night he was wounded. She remembered the day he would not let her heal a deep cut in his hand, wrapping it in an old shirt, never letting her see the wound until it had scarred over completely. Convinced he'd come to rescue her and take her to the snowy peaks, to this beautiful land where their child would be born, and many more would follow, she hardly felt the terrible blow that sent her plummeting into the cold depths.

A week later, on a stormy night, the lighthouse lantern was blown out and remained unlit for a couple of days. Intrigued, the fisherman's friends decided to find out what had happened. They found the door sealed completely with several wooden planks. Quickly, they pulled one of the planks, using it as a lever to remove the rest of them and free the way into the tower. They found dark traces of dried blood in the staircase, but no sign of him. As they were climbing, the bloodstains diminished, and the last steps seemed dusty. They picked up some heteroclite objects that appeared to have been thrown, a broken cup, pencils, mostly sheets of paper. At the top, the windows were open to the tempest and the floor littered with scattered papers and manuscripts covered with an irregular handwriting. Everything, the walls, the chairs, the tables and the windowsills were dusty with flakes of fine white down.

NOOR EL QAMAR

I was discovered on a misty night by a drunken sailor: a bundle glowing by the prow, on top of folded sails. Bewildered, the man stumbled over a thick, glistening rope dangling out of nowhere. As he held the plaited silk, it slipped from his hands and vanished almost instantly, but not before he glimpsed swirls of fire moving up and down a radiant ladder. He looked again at the light and dared not come closer. "It's a piece of the moon," he said, "Noor! Noor!" and retreated to the farthest end of the small fishing boat.

For days and nights I glowed in the hazy mists, illuminating the dark crested waves for a great distance. Motionless, the man stared and stared until his barge landed safely upon these shores. It is recounted that he kept repeating, "Noor el Qamar, Noor el Qamar," which in his dialect—that of people from lands where Shams, the sun, begins his daily journey—means light of the moon. Then, the sailor withdrew into profound silence and disappeared in the Djebel mountains, or at least that is what I have been told.

Of what became of me at that time, of what my life was like during that remote past I only know from other peoples' accounts. This is how I retrace the first stages of my life in this world. For I only conceived precise memories from the day I used language to communicate. Before, I kept alive a kaleidoscope of images and indefinable sensations.

Some things I recall distinctly. I understood from the very beginning I was expected to close my eyes at night, and play dead at sunset the way others did. Later, I learned this was called sleep, a normal activity necessary for humans, which I feigned in order to withdraw into myself, shielded from my surroundings. It enabled me to retreat and relive the events, images and sounds of previous days. With time, I developed an infallible memory. I'd try to discover the mysterious mechanisms of dreams, which were never allotted to me, meditating on one shape, one thought. I only experienced haunting visions of clinging to a monumental breast, and the pain of letting go. I'd see myself clutching at the gigantic curves enveloping me, my mouth gorged with soft warmth, then ruthlessly hurled into a cold void.

In these early days of my earthly experience, I was entrusted to the care of the highest ranked inhabitant in the region—a privilege inherited by their descendants. All considered me a daughter of the moon, though the radiance I first so strongly emitted had gradually faded; it nevertheless lasted innumerable years, causing people to believe I possessed supernatural powers. To this day, centuries later, whenever I remain in absolute darkness, an ethereal aura emanates from me.

Since I reached maidenhood, I have scarcely changed. I was and am still to this day, fair and pale, not ivory pale, for ivory is hard and my skin and flesh give the impression of being hollow and vacuous as if formed by condensed mists. My long hair seems to be made of the same substance; its swaying waves mold themselves to my body as if my skin were a magnet.

They called me Lena, among many other names of lesser importance. One day, tall men from distant lands came in search of Moona, a moon Goddess they identified with me. To this day, the polemic around what should be my official name is still forceful. The High Priests favor Lena though most people call me Noor since it was the first name ever given to me by the common folks and it is my favorite. As many in the village, especially the elders, revered me as a Goddess, I was forbidden to take a husband. My features were carved in wood and magical stones like moonstones. Small effigies were kept on altars in every household, continuously lit by oil lamps. The rivers I bathed in and the fields I walked through were considered miraculous. The inhabitants withdrew religiously when I approached a stream or a riverbank, allowing me a welcomed privacy. I usually sat or walked, awaiting sunset. When colors faded in the sky, I entered the water, marveling at the language of the ripples bathed in moonlight.

Many pilgrims came to fetch water and grain from our region, which prospered with the visitors' flow. Women, especially brides suffering from infertility, stood in line, begging me to bless scented oil flasks with which they'd faithfully anoint their sterile wombs. Worshipped and looked after with deference, yet suffering from an indescribable anxiety, that of being lonely and different, I doubted my wisdom and holiness, dedicating my solitary nights to study. I have now compiled all existing volumes and treatises about mysticism, astrology, and esoteric religions in order to discover the mystery of my origin and destiny. I often think of the silk ladder the sailor described.

Obsessed with recovering my lost innocence, I have chanced upon legends and myths about the Chosen People, those who after proper initiation are allowed, every fifty years, to sail on a given time and at a place indicated by the position of the stars. When they'd reach the secret location of the stellar configuration, the silk ladder descends into their boat and they climb it to milk the moon, bringing back the secret of wisdom and eternal life. But so far I have not encountered any tangible proof of this, my only hope to follow the Chosen People's path.

Indeed, time has no bearing upon me. I have stopped counting years. I do not have the consolation of remembering past lives as a reward for purity and rituals. Therefore, I am confronted with the mystery of my origin, convinced or perhaps wishing I had previous incarnations. Here, I live a paradox between the continuity of my own life and the successive lives of the once-born people. In this eternal present, my implacable memory weighs heavily on me. Forced to assume the monotony of sameness, I helplessly witness others live and die endlessly. In the chanting and speech of the living I recognize old phrases, inflexions of voices, tonalities of those long gone. Around me, I see fragments, features, eyes, eyebrows, gestures, attitudes, and even expressions. Every person I look at is a composite of those I have previously known.

During the long solitary and sleepless nights of my childhood, I studied people's expectations and trained myself to behave accordingly. As no one believed I had emotions, I learned to control them. It took me several lifetimes—of once-born people's lives—to learn not to shed a tear and maintain the monochord tone of voice that now characterizes me. But that training is only a memory. Now, I live alone in the Temple except for the succeeding generations of families in charge of my well-being. They reside in a secluded aisle, never disturbing me, never approaching me unless called upon. Aside from maintaining the hearth fire on a stone altar in the winter months, they keep a tray of fresh water and food covered with fine linen.

The Temple, with its high pillars, was erected a hundred years after my arrival at the top of a hill overlooking the village so its inhabitants would feel comforted and protected by my presence. Its location was carefully chosen so that astrologers could observe the waxing moon from all directions. On annual festivities such as the solstice, villagers and pilgrims walk by me in processions, kneeling, touching my bare feet for benediction. I sit, statuesque, on a throne-like chair for long hours, surrounded by the High Priests. These ceremonies tire me because I know the futility behind it all and feel as helpless as the petitioners, if not more. All this time is irremediably lost, spent away from my search for the right time to sail as one of the Chosen People.

Because no one knows I do not sleep, I work and meditate intensely at night. Seated by the circular font that stands in open air in the middle of the Temple, I watch the moon's alabaster face. Night after night I engage in a mute dialogue with its changing phases, dialogue that never leaves me satisfied. Musing under a full moon, I, Noor el Qamar, called daughter of the moon, yearn for a mother, or a sister in that distant, unreachable globe. But faith has never forsaken me and during all stages of the pregnant moon, I run unnoticed towards the secret paths leading to the shore where I keep a boat ready to sail. On nights like these, uncontrollable visions of a silk ladder stretching towards the fountain come to me, and I see myself retracing the movements of the fall, disappearing in the depths of an intangible breast. I hear no voices, recall no faces, yet I sense the visions are messages of a kind of birthright.

With imaginary fingers, I caress the configurations of the glowing orb, wondering if I had been rejected for having human form. Were there others like me somewhere? Were the swirls of fire envisioned by the sailor trying to rescue me or had they abandoned me to my fate? Legends say that ideal conditions for sailing in search of the ladder happen only once in a human's lifetime. Will I ever accept my condition of eternal longing, or will I attempt to end it out of boredom and despair? I see people die of diseases, wounds, poisoning and old age but I am never ill. Whenever brambles scratch my skin, my flesh heals immediately, exuding a hazy, albescent fluid instead of a viscous scarlet matter. Was I a human child bathed in moon dust as some legends recall? With time, I trained myself to experience human sensations, imagining pain, cold and heat. As a result, I have lost touch with my inherent nature.

Many generations have seen me as a mature woman and no one alive has any memory of my slow evolution. My childhood belongs to a mythical time when forests covered most of the land and rivers ran different courses. Changes, although slight, give me a tenuous hope that even if I do not reach my goal, there will be an end to my torment. Besides soothing, unifying visions, I also experience terrifying glimpses of myself, old and wrinkled like parchment, unable to climb the long sought for ladder. I see my decrepit self disintegrate, collapse into ashes upon reaching the last rung, in particles of dying light.

A witness for centuries to a life I could not share, I came to believe I would never know what it is like to be with a mortal man. Aside from my serving attendants no one was ever allowed to come near me outside the ritual; no one, except once, so long ago that I do not trust my recollections. As seasons shift irrevocably, in constant renewal, it seems to me as if it were a story I have read or a legend I have interwoven out of fragmented bits and pieces, some of which did not even belong to me. It all began when the High Priests commissioned a local sculptor named Shahir to carve my face on top of the Temple's main stone pillars. They also ordered a monumental marble statue destined to be placed in the foothills by the mosaic baths where many ceremonies were held. He came daily to the Temple, setting scrolls of parchment papers on an easel and spent hours sketching as I sat or stood immobile by the fountain. He did not seem to be aware of my presence. He would barely glance at me, absorbed in his own creations. I recall his hands, incessantly moving and my awe upon seeing his three-dimensional sketches. It was like discovering a twin sister as mute and remote as the one I might have had.

After these sessions, I felt estranged, eager to see the result of his work, eager to exchange a few words with him. I took long walks around the countryside, followed at a distance by my maidservant, until I discovered the quarry where Shahir spent most of his days. His broad shoulders and muscular chest shone in the bright light as he painstakingly fashioned the hard stone. He looked at me then with an intensity that unsettled me, for everyone else bowed their heads or faced me with an empty look. I grew accustomed to watching him struggle as his tools unveiled shining, unexpected shapes, observing his fingers run along a curve, rub the grain of the stone until it acquired the texture of skin and silk. I waited patiently until he would sit next to me, even for a brief moment. To this day, his dark brown eyes and his smile cross my mind, fleeting images, often punctuated by the echoes of his constant hammering on stone. He never allowed me to see all of his sculptures. The marble statue would probably never be completed, he once confided. I did not understand why.

We left together one day, without exchanging a word until we reached the mountain thickets. We came upon a cave in which we rested, how long, it is impossible to determine for I envision only one long night. I know he would not have survived the cold unless he held me close in the darkness, my long hair enveloping us. Unable to sleep, accustomed to long vigils, I tried to imagine what a mortal woman would feel and sensed that the very absence of images I experienced with Shahir had to be what humans call happiness. He wanted to spend the rest of his life with me, far away from the village and the Temple walls; he would take me across the seas where no one would ever find us. We lived on berries and nuts. He occasionally hunted as we moved constantly, fearful of staying too long in the same place. Careless of leaving tracks, he would carve my face on trees, on the frigid porous cave walls, marking stones, or small branches. It all seemed to me as one extended day and night until we met a small community of people who spoke a language unknown to us. This nomadic tribe led their sheep across different pastures and very seldom settled for long in a given area. They welcomed us, allowing us to share their lives, convinced that I would bring protection upon them.

Deep inside, I feared my presence would harm Shahir in some way and that our closeness might be detrimental to him. He dreamed of reaching a land beyond the sea where he could unearth shapeless forms buried within delicately veined marble, awaiting his stiletto and chisel. In the meantime, he explored the possibilities of the forests, discovering the grain and texture of wood, creating vessels the shepherds could use, bringing life to the porous granite concretions in the numerous caves we encountered in the region. His touch, the pressure of his hands, I still feel on my skin as he, day after day, reshaped the dunes of my nakedness. Eyes closed, I would visualize him at the quarry, endlessly smoothing the fold of an ear lobe, of a pleated veil, until the glistening marble came to life under his fingertips.

I saw Shahir grow tired, his shoulders bend as time left its imprint upon him. He gradually changed, his face losing its former glow, yet his eyes always lighting his entire expression. His body, no longer full nor strong, never ceased to be an extension of my own. We could not stay apart. How long did it last? I cannot say for sure: until we refused to move further with the successive tribes we encountered, until he said he wanted to die in our village. Death was coming to him. He knew it. I could not face losing him. Unable to give him strength, I felt my youth was useless. He insisted we initiate the journey home. He wanted to see his sculptures again, especially the unfinished ones.

When we arrived, we hardly recognized the village. It had spread out, houses mushrooming everywhere. I went to the Temple where the servants surrounded me, bewildered, as if I were an apparition. All were unknown to me, including the High Priests. They had waited for my return, preserving my cult intact according to the elders' instructions, keeping oil lamps lit day and night in the sacred chamber, as it had been done for generations. Shahir's sculpture was erected by the Temple's front gate. I saw myself trapped in translucent marble, my long hair, my back, hands and feet anchored to the stone, struggling to free myself as one caught in quicksand. I understood Shahir's words. He saw me as I really was, helpless, unable to escape my destiny, forbidden to share his fate. We looked intently into each other's eyes.

The High Priests seemed relieved at seeing me. Many ailments and plagues had occurred during my long absence. They prayed for my blessing and wisdom, bowing as they joined their palms beneath their forehead, hoping I would not abandon them again. No one recognized Shahir in the old man accompanying me. Later, I was told the story of the famous artist who had created this incomparable alabaster-like statue. Madly in love with his model, he disappeared in the mountains. It had happened so long ago, no one remembered the details. Signs of his passage are still found occasionally in caves or tree trunks on which he immortalized the face of Noor, the daughter of the moon. No one knew what became of him. My absence was considered a bad omen followed by a recrudescence of the cult through purification rituals. The people hoped I would return, possibly by sea, as I had once been discovered.

No one questioned the presence of an old, dying man in the sacred Temple. They referred to him as the Wise One. Our intimacy had somewhat extended Shahir's life, although we will never know how long we lived in the distant mountains, nor how long he remained by my side throughout my sleepless nights, both of us unaware of the passing of time. When he died in my arms, I was unable to cry.

I have been entrusted with the sacred book of Vukshsak. It is so old, and dry, no one ever dares touch its leaves—impalpable, as butterfly's wings. The High Priests taught me the secret way of handling the Vukshsak with a special velvet cloth lined with silk similar to the one that sheathes its cover. Whenever a prediction is to be made, I open the book at random while staring at the implorer's eyes because it is believed that a person's energy dictates his own fate. Then, I interpret the signs and symbols according to tradition. After the reading, the sacred book rests in a special niche protected by glass, in the Temple's main altar.

I wish someone would read the Vukshsak for me and disclose the propitious time. Full moon after full moon, my boat is ready to sail. I run barefoot in the sand, heart pounding, confident my calculations are correct this time, running until it is too late: In a fraction of a second the moon's face is upturned, the ladder pulled. Until the next pregnant moon, I confine myself to meditations, torn by recurring visions of birth and death, of a long sleepless night. In my lonely quest, I, Noor el Qamar, light of the moon, seated near the circular fountain, feed upon the sight of the alabaster orb, and await a sign, a change in the eternal dialogue with the multiple-shaped Goddess, hopeful of having the ladder sent forth to me, to the foot of the Temple's fountain.

THE CURE

I can't remember precisely when it first started. All I know is that I felt a growth deep inside, invading my whole being, carving me up like a ripe, helpless fruit, gnawing me to the bones. I could not name the disease. In order to ease the pain, I changed my diet, avoided alcohol for a while and tried a variety of useless remedies. During that period I managed to circumscribe the area of discomfort by keeping constantly busy and active. As soon as I'd slow down, It would reach my arms, my legs, numbing my extremities. Luckily, I had few idle moments. At the time I was the editor of *Digressions,* a multi-disciplinary publication that absorbed me entirely. I remember shuffling constantly between deadlines. When friends showed some concern about the way I looked, I would explain that the puffiness around my eyes, my swollen face, resulted from lack of sleep. "I need a vacation," I kept repeating.

I consulted an internist a few months later, and after a thorough examination followed by a series of tests, he reassured me with a smile: "There's absolutely nothing wrong with you. Report to me at the end of the month." He scribbled on a small piece of paper while saying, "Here. Take one tablet after each meal. They should make a difference. If not . . . I might consider further exploration." After several visits to other specialists, I shunned doctors, presumptuous healers of body and mind, aware by then that whatever was taking possession of me thrived upon dreams and emotions. I sensed I could destroy It, outsmart It, provided I worked incessantly, drowning instantly all unconscious, incipient images.

No one suspected my internal struggle, though the being within me, needing more space, proliferated insidiously, until It spread into my limbs, throwing fine shoots between my toes, in places where skin offers the least resistance, the way my dying willow desperately sprouts a profusion of green leaves from its base. One morning, terrified, using sharp blades, I severed the protruding presence like an unwanted corn. From then on, self-conscious of every inch of my skin, every orifice, I became skilled at constant self-mutilation. Alert, I spent hours daily in my boudoir like a courtesan, anointing myself before my public appearance, emulating Josephine de Beauharnais' or Cleopatra's ritual baths.

At night, I'd stare at the ceiling in the penumbra, feel my veins fill with a now familiar fluid, paralyzing and cold, like Freon, etherizing me at times, the next minute causing me to sweat and swell, forcing me to open windows and turn the buzzing fan on full speed to hover like a predator above my bed. Night after night I would initiate an active dialogue with It. I resisted naming It, yet I knew It to be more akin to myself than my own reflection in the mirror. A faceless, alien being was taking over, converting my old familiar self into a carcass, an empty discarded carapace. I was being expelled like a molting coat, the way too tight gloves start cracking at the seams, outgrown by a swollen hand. Would anyone notice—despite my red alert, my constant vigils—through the minuscule crevices and fissures I scrutinized in a magnifying glass, that I was harboring a dry elephant skin, hardened like thick crackled bark, crying out, ready to be exposed at the slightest neglect?

I avoided being around people, feeling as uncomfortable in a group as with an individual. Whenever I was invited to see a play or to have lunch, I always found a pretext, either that I had an emergency, a last-minute piece to deliver, anything that would occur to me to evade more questions. Many must have speculated about what was going on in my life.

When I ran into my friend Jen in a bookstore downtown, she asked, "What's with you, lately?"

"Not much. Nothing new. And you?"

"Let's have lunch this week," she said, "I can't talk here."

"It is going to be difficult. I'm trying to juggle . . . "

"OK," she interrupted, "I'm awfully busy too. Summer is high season for us. Can't complain. But you must find time for friends, you know."

"Jen. You don't understand. I can't seem to get caught up, that's all."

"I must go. I have a closing at two," she said hurriedly, looking at her wrist-watch. "Listen, Vanessa, you don't need to tell me if you don't want to, but you 'are' seeing someone, aren't you?"

I forced myself to smile, relieved by her departure. Seeing someone? Why did Jen's question seem so incongruous? I realized I couldn't remember the last time I went out on a date. And worse, I didn't even miss it. Men's attention was the least of my concerns. Was I always that way? I remember the days when I'd be shattered when I was alone for a long time. Better to let Jen think something was going on. Anything seemed better than revealing the misery

I was going through. At that point, I could hardly sleep and was feeling totally helpless. It was as though at night, I'd step into another dimension, in which I was either immensely happy or on the verge of suicide. Never before had my dreams been so vivid, leaving me troubled when I'd wake up, unable to recapture scenes and faces that a moment ago seemed so real. But that uneasiness didn't last. Quickly my attention was drawn to that unbearable growth within me and I feared something horrible would happen. Despite my efforts, I worried how much longer my skin would sustain the illusion of wholeness and be able to resist such relentless pressure.

Distressed, I decided to trace the one man who could help me in my unspeakable calamity, knowing that relocating him would not be a simple endeavor. Cabeza, as we used to call him, was a Peruvian anthropologist with whom I had participated several years ago in an expedition in the Yucatan peninsula. I wrote articles for the *New Yorker* at that time. Yes, I thought, that made sense because lots of details surrounding that period seemed to evade me, as if belonging to another, foreign to me. In an odd way, I suspected my problem might have originated in that area and that our guide would have the answers to my questions. He was a complex, charismatic character, well ahead of his time, although he seemed to live in a mythical past.

Cabeza. He was not really old. Maybe in his fifties, but his white hair, falling over the nape of his neck, rare and thinning on top, conferred on him an aura, a dignified appearance. His singular blue eyes were most of the time hidden behind lightly tinted lenses. Members of the group grew fond of him. I immediately felt at home as we walked under the gigantic green canopy on narrow, meandering paths Cabeza's assistants continuously cleared for us with their machetes. After the initial wonderment, stepping upon ancient stones seemed natural; I'd wander about them with the confidence of retracing a former playground. Even the numerous and complex birdcalls became surprisingly familiar. I often recall the magical glyphs carved on the Mayan temples' walls and how Cabeza deciphered them, bringing the mute ruins to life. Later, as our group sat around a camp fire, he would unravel the everyday rhythms of old cities, his tales interspersed with scenes of bloody rituals. He often motioned his hands as if writing or drawing in the evening air. He believed virtual reality experiments had been discovered prior to modern technology and hinted at his own initiation by survivors of extinct tribes. The rest of the trip I remember as in a dream. Cabeza had said to me one night: "Learn to forget what is detrimental to your soul. If you do not, you will never be in control of your destiny."

I never quite understood his words. In retrospect, I sensed that he wanted me to channel my memories in a direction he alone could visualize. What did he know about me that pre-occupied him so much? We often lay outside in our hammocks under the constelled sky as he improvised speeches somehow addressed to each of the stars as well as to each of us individually, making us feel as though we had lived before in that land and participated in the remote lives he conjured up. His raucous voice resonated in the silence, punctuated by the strident cries of nocturnal birds of prey. He paused at times, as if lost in thought, uttering words in an inaudible tone, then resumed his lecture at the original pace. Never before had I experienced such sense of belonging. Images arose, flowing in my mind as if coming from a deeper consciousness. These recollections seemed in some strange fashion to lessen my pain, while at the same time provoking sporadic bouts of fever, which left me completely exhausted. I suspect some seed or pollen, carried by the cool breezes, along with mysterious scents or burnt herbs or spices used in our daily meals, surrounded us, penetrating our lungs, lingering on our clothes, covering our pores. Could an unfathomable presence have traveled back with us incognito from that time on? I do not recall how deeply I breathed as I faced the cold temples' walls, how often I ran my fingers over carved images and sculptures, possibly reenacting a ceremonial gesture that triggered the release of unleashed powers. I had often heard of the Pharaoh's curse. Perhaps a malevolent force was directed against those intruding upon Mayan ruins. Had Cabeza profaned their sacred stones by revealing too much to us?

When I finally got in touch with him, I caught the first plane to Washington, D. C., where he was attending a conference on the exploitation of Brazilian gold mines and its disastrous effect on the indigenous population. I was to meet him at the front door of the Hyatt Regency. I found him pacing the lobby, head bent, his eternal sunglasses giving him the semblance of a blind man. He seemed tired but quite unchanged, wearing the familiar rumpled linen shirt. He looked at me without seeing me. A moment later, we talked as if we had been together the day before. After listening to me, shaking his head occasionally, he suggested we go to a nearby sidewalk café. There, we sat on the terrace under a red striped awning. He explained his concerns about the survival of the remaining tribes in the Amazon and, for a while, seemed oblivious to my problems.

"Tell me everything again," he said abruptly, taking his glasses off. His blue eyes almost darkened as he stared at me.

For a second, I felt immersed in a kaleidoscope of images fading and arising in me, enfolding as fractals constantly entwined within their fragmented mirror image. I wanted to stop that incontrollable, dizzying movement, focus as in a close-up on the fraction of second linked with a sense of intense pleasure invading me all over with a warm presence: a body linked to mine suddenly dissolving into bright colors swirling, leaving me inert, engulfing me into dark whirlwinds sucking me as in the eye of a storm. I took a deep breath, remembering why I had come here. Nervous, I described my struggle, my fears; how It had become intolerable. He did not interrupt me and kept rubbing his chin in concentration.

"That's all," I said. I tasted my coffee. It was cold. I pushed it aside. "So, what do you think?"

He shook his head and remained silent, scrutinizing the gold rim of his empty cup.

"Vanessa," he then said, "I say you might improve." He pursed his lips. "However . . . I don't say I foresee a complete recovery." He lifted his eyebrows and rested his chin on his fist.

"But what is it that's happening to me? What is It?" I'm not sure, but I believe I almost yelled.

Cabeza ignored me completely, deeply absorbed in his thoughts. Seeing my desolate look, he ordered: "Write, now. Write everything I'm going to tell you. Here is what you will have to do," he said, clearing his throat.

I started taking notes as he gave me specific instructions. He recommended plastic surgery as a palliative for any visible protrusion. I should constantly work at repairing any fissure of my skin, as minimal as it might be. He would send me a list of incantations and excerpts of meditations to keep my vigil hours intense with optimal intellectual activity. Meanwhile, I was to study the four *Vedas*, the *Kama Sutra*, Sufi philosophy, the *Kabala*, the *Dead Sea Scrolls*, the *Collected Works of Paracelsus* and his analysis of Marsilio Ficino's *Book of Life*, Erasmus' *Praise of Folly*, the complete works of Jung and Freud without forgetting Lacan, as many utopias as I could encounter, Saint John of the Cross's mystical poems, Arabic erotic *Kasaid*, mystical Sufi verse, and all the poetry I could acquire. I should preferably read all works in the original. He recommended a trip to Alaska, the planning of a series of articles about Eskimos and the bright dancing Northern Lights. I was to study the breeding behavior of horned puffins, those black seabirds with white chests and undersides, also called sea parrots on account of their red and yellow beaks. I would enjoy watching the courtship rituals of these seabirds that mate for life before nesting in rock crevices and sea cliffs, where they hide in small holes like troglodytes. I was to meditate and take long solitary walks in the wilderness as a preparation for my next expedition in the Argentinean pampas where I was to share the gauchos' life and produce a documentary focusing on the connection between their daily consumption of Yerba Mate, and their immunity to certain diseases. According to some beliefs, the mate enabled Argentineans to develop an outrageous ability to engulf tons of red meat without any risk of cancer. Cabeza highly recommended drinking mate on regular basis. I was to maintain the habit of these endless walks initiated in Alaska, until I lost the remotest illusion of ever reaching the distant horizon. He also recommended I explore the Way of the Shamans, presumably capable of addressing my unwelcome presence, convincing It to release me from this unbearable torture, just as they assist agonizing people, exhorting their indecisive souls to depart. I should rely upon these wise old men. Cabeza stopped, rubbed his chin insistently, and paused. He then added some special fumigation to the list. Finally, he explained I should perform a ceremony at a certain time each month. As the waning moon thinned into a faint crescent, I was to circle three times around a bonfire lighted with The One Thousand Precious Roots, some of which he promised to gather for me.

In answer to my unformulated question, he denied vehemently any part in fathering the monster.

"To keep It quiet," he said, "I'll send you a case of a special brew, mixed with Caipirinia, Pisco, Raki, Arak and Armagnac. Drink a shot before and after meals in case of extreme discomfort and the symptoms should subside. I will also include unguents to keep your skin supple, resisting attacks from within or without. No new clefts will be created.

"You will have won the major battle! No one will suspect the depth of your suffering, but keep an eye on your natural orifices. These must be under continuous close observation. Wash five times a day, and after your ablutions, spray thoroughly with an infusion of eucalyptus, rosemary, mint, lavender and lilac, all in equal proportions. Use it the same way one uses a mosquito repellent. It will remain subdued as if in a cocoon. Nothing is too much work if you want a beautiful rose garden," he added in a meditative tone. "Consider yourself a rose! A little pain, such great results. . . . And you will bloom for as long as you keep up your fight. I have never let down any expedition member. Never. Remember, it is during night that one gathers strength for the daily battle, as it is thanks to the sun's warmth that one does not fear obscurity."

"Now," said Cabeza, resting both palms on the table, "I must go. But here, note my next address. It may take months, maybe years, to reach me in the Tibetan monasteries, but you have my instructions and will receive a package shortly with what I have promised."

We both stood. His arm rested around my shoulders. I could feel the pressure of his fingers sinking into my flesh.

"Are you leaving now?" he asked.

"Soon. I'll have another espresso first."

He nodded in assent. Back turned, he waved goodbye, his mind already deploring the tragedy of the ill-fated natives along the Amazon river. His hair, strikingly white in the sunshine, made him look much older. I watched him walk slowly through the terrace, his figure gradually fading from view. I did not know what to think as I glanced at the thick black leather notebook in which I had rapidly written everything as he spoke. Spellbound, I felt like taking the next flight to Tibet to be near him. I would heal faster by his side, but I knew I had to go to Alaska and Argentina, and perhaps in those places, I would find the answer to the many questions I dared not ask. I thought of Psyche, her impossible tasks and wondered whether I'd chance upon eagles, ants, friendly hands to guide me in that cryptic labyrinth hidden in my briefcase.

Back home, I worked incessantly, trying to leave my apartment in order. I had to go through tons of correspondence and endless filing. This activity helped control It. There was no spare time for It to breed on fleeting images or emotions. In addition, I had already started a routine combining mental and corporeal exercises. I packed with care, beginning with my favorite and indispensable books, aware that my absence could be prolonged indefinitely. I rediscovered old, misplaced ones and found myself reading underlined passages. Leafing through poems by Eluard, one of my favorite poets, I was surprised to find a few handwritten, long-forgotten words. I stood still for a while, unable to breathe, my veins and arteries emptying, shrinking. Scribbled all over the pages, among Eluard's cries of despair, words I had never said, but like seeds, once grew within me as inside a greenhouse, creating an illusion of luminous foliage and exotic petals.

Some letters stood out, as if dripping with fresh blood: Mauro. I was never alone in Mérida. Mauro was always next to me at the sites, during the meals, in the buses; his hammock always hung close to mine. Back then, I could not envision a single day without him. . . . His dark eyes lit up his whole face as he talked about his plans. Everything seemed so simple, listening to him. He had joined those men who crossed by cable from one mountain side to another to reach distant, inaccessible villages. He dreamed of improving their living conditions. These missions were scheduled twice a week. I could never watch their flight over the vertiginous precipice. I kept busy those days classifying records or helping with the camp's daily chores. One night, Mauro was late. He did not join us for supper. They said it was a defective bolt . . . nobody's fault. I wanted to die. Cabeza took care of me then. Some things I vaguely recalled. I could see Cabeza praying and burning incense while I lay in bed. Mauro. How I yearned for the flesh of his flesh, the child he could no longer give me! As if knowing It had no father, the creature grew formless, wanting my life in revenge. I relived the days following my return from Yucatan. It was much later that, like a woman about to give birth, I became only aware of what

I carried in my belly. It took years to develop into that unbearable weight.

What had Cabeza done? Should I be grateful to him or resent his intrusion in my life? These speculations intensified the pain, filing It, sharpening It like a thousand blades. I felt an urge to insult him, tell him he had deceived me. Yet I liked the cure I was about to undertake, knowing I would never be totally freed, somehow convinced so much was already inscribed in the temples' walls. From then on, like a mother-to-be, eternally concealing the fruit of her passion, I would follow Mauro daily, his smile, the shadow of his steps, hear his laughter over and over again. I would recapture every minute we shared with no fear of It destroying me because I had Cabeza's cure.

SEARCH

He tried to put words together in an alchemy of signs, colors and smells. He, the last depository of knowledge, who had served for years at many courts, in innumerable past lives, was now losing face when confronted with his personal quest. He wasn't close to creating the original potion, the filter long sought for in centuries of dreams and unformulated hopes.

All he ever obtained was a paraphrase, a redundancy of three simple words: "I love you," or "I love myself," the difference being so tiny, the formulas so identical that all it took was one double binding broken loose, a rise in temperature, an imbalance of catalytic elements, and either the reflexive was obtained, or the displacement between wording and initial meaning was lost in the process.

The proper mixture seemed unstable, unattainable, unfathomable and unpredictable, the way a delicate perfume decomposes over certain skins when mixed with pore secretions, adulterating the initial scent. The original formula, he decided, had been lost since time immemorial, leading to confusing myths such as people drowning into their own reflection, making love to their own creation, or confronted with arrows becoming boomerangs with a mind of their own, defying all laws of gravity.

Perplexed, he caressed his long, well-groomed beard, indulging in long pensive strokes. He spent most of his time in a high-ceilinged room amid crystal phials, long-necked flasks, and multi-shaped copper alembics. In the largest alembic, facing his voluminous desk, water constantly traveled through darkness as inside a whale's belly, distilled over rose petals or orange blossoms, rising with heat faster than over magic carpets.

He concentrated on the wingless molecules, imagining they'd give him a clue as to his constant concern, replacing them with words and letters. He visualized the vapor's voyage through the alembic's cold bent neck, as if through translucent glass, imagining the broken processions of letters, the various modalities of their regrouping. He saw them swell, expand in the limited space, then condense into streaming ribbons pouring steadily out of the funnel.

But unlike words, molecules, in their sacrificial flight, disgregated and reorganized in unison, obeying rigid laws, always in the same order. He kept performing his mental distillation, writing and rewriting, confident he'd find the right solution. Something was defying his observation, an imperceptible detail he knew he was close to discovering. All he required was time and patience; the former, never denied to him, the latter, fading away, failing him day after day.

Discouraged, he then decided to improvise. He dreamed of fluid words reducing the whole perception into an eternal instant. He invented with great eagerness and a sense of premeditated success, an invisible ink responding to rigid codes, indecipherable except to readers possessing intuitively similar decoding systems. In other words, a language for minorities, almost a wordless message as those from the heart, only to be read by someone experiencing the exact same feeling, or perhaps by owners of special magnifying iridium glasses.

He gradually came to the conclusion that his attempts would remain fruitless. Words, phrases, spoiled by memory, which added layers of meanings, and by conditioned reflexes, intensifying or diminishing the initial message, altering its fleeting content, were unable to be harnessed in a carcanet of labels. It was as if he tried to possess beauty or life in its extemporaneity—the way some stuff exotic bluebirds—or pretend to preserve the transitory purity of the shadow of reeds above a river or stream. The brush of petals over skin, he thought, meant more than elaborate cogitation and displays of eloquence.

He finally accepted his faith. Living in a world of mutability, of free emotions, harnessed only for a brief instant, lasting more than eternity, he realized time elapsed destroyed the immediacy of experience. Erasing layers of memory allowed an impression of novelty, a sense of wonderment, the forever possible amazement linked to the unknown. And what were the conditions for newness of experience, he reflected, genuine ignorance, or partial forgetfulness?

He smoothed his silky beard. Hum . . . yet another elixir to search for, in addition to the others. Feeling always one step behind, no matter what he experienced or discovered, he realized that words seemed to resist the ferrets of specificity, escaping the initial thought, emotion or perception. Like oversized gloves, or those becoming useless over swelled fingers, words no longer fit the meaning, and the most difficult to harness, love, could never coexist harmoniously in combination with others. Its vivid and elusive nature reminded him of mercury. He closed his eyes and recalled his experiments with the gliding silvery substance, breaking lose at the least touch into infinitely small particles, bubbles of scintillating water, schools of shimmering silver fish.

IV

TELL ME, MAYRA

"No one asked me to lift the baby. It cried and cried in that deserted office, filling corridors with a disturbing presence. I was only a few steps away from the half-open door impelling me to enter. Behind the desk, the tiny crib stood on the chair as if its habitual occupant had shrunk from his prepotency into this helpless newborn crying to the point of choking. It all happened so fast, Mayra. I set aside the light cotton blanket, uncovering a naked and soaked, almost premature baby. I took the small creature in my cupped hands and ran to the nearest sink. From then on, it happened too fast, as if it weren't real, as if I were witnessing someone who looked like me performing in my place. I'm scared, Mayra."

"Calm down, child. Fear is a gust of cold wind you must not allow in your mind or heart. The way torrential storms ruthlessly invade fragile houses, fear's whirling eddies will possess you, penetrating through the least fissures. Secure doors and windows, open the shutters and let *The Sun*'s rays warm your heart. See here, in the Arcanum *The World*, how the young maiden smiles alone in the center of an oval crown? Look closely and see how tightly woven is the braided wheat wreath framing her, protecting her from all winged creatures, stallions, falcons, lions, even from angels. Like her, retreat into your center. See the symmetry of *The Ace of Coins?* You belong right there, in the inner circle of the stylized Tree of Life. Open the eyes of the soul and tell what you see inside."

"The baby slipped, disappearing into the sink hole. I held on to his feet and pulled him back into my arms but his head was split in two, the way the sectioned top of a half-boiled egg hangs, still attached to the shell. The upper part of his skull fell, dangling from the scalp. I immediately put it back in place, heart leaping out of my chest, and closed my eyes. I can't say how long I stood, an immobile sleepwalker, praying it was a nightmare, counting my heartbeat, until the baby moaned and cried faintly. I dried his soft skin with my silk skirt and hurried back to the crib. He seemed perfectly normal, pink and rosy, comforted at last, and slept almost instantly as I rearranged the smooth blanket around him. I left the office rapidly that day without anyone taking notice of me. You see, Mayra, why I had to see you urgently? I'm not even sure it happened. Tell me, Mayra, was it a dream?"

"You question me as though I held the key. I only read the figures spread out on the table, lined up at your request. I'll try to help you solve this riddle. Remember that spoken words project shadows, circling in their own dance, notes echoing each other, bringing things to pass. Place your hand on the Tarot deck. Let it rest a while. Take a deep breath. Allow your energy to penetrate the cards, to connect with the major Arcana. Now, over the black velvet, deep as a starless night gravid with the moon's crescent, I will unfold the silken and gilded images, disclosing the unseen and unknown. Now, you will see clearly into yourself." "Before you start, let me tell you, Mayra. I thought I'd die at the sight of the split head. I wished I could exchange my life for his, wished I'd never touched that crib. No one will ever know I was there, yet, since then, I have found no rest, no respite. What if there were sequels later on? What if in his adolescent years, the child was to experience headaches, memory loss, or worse? Just because I wanted to help where I was not needed. You were right, Mayra, when you warned me to stay away from *The Ace of Cups* with its rustling fountain echoing a nearby spring. The sink. I shouldn't have gone near the sink."

"Wait, child! Hush. Cut, and let the Tarot speak. See the Arcanum called *The Star*? The naked woman filling water from the spring with two earthenware jugs? She brings life, delivers dreams from door to door, one jug well balanced on her head, the other on the shoulder. She is your destiny: the virgin midwife. You can walk by reedy shores provided you do not seek the Sight in the mirror pool whenever unstirred by winds. Following the paths of running streams and rivulets, you will hear echoing dreams. But remember, I have said this before, stay away from *The Lover*. You have neither past nor future with him. Your life is connected to water, flowing water."

"How could I be a midwife destroying life, Mayra? I wanted to run pure water over the soiled skin, hold the baby against my breast and comfort him. I couldn't bear to hear him cry. Then I saw myself as this ruthless woman brandishing a weapon, unsheathing its shiny blade, *The Queen of Swords*, as those witches stealing newborns for black masses, or, throwing a rope around their necks, enslaving them as the twin boys chained in *The Devil*, here below. You know, Mayra, I've acted out of good will, I only tried to help. How can I account for such clumsiness? I remember his head cracking like a porcelain doll. Was it really me, Mayra?"

"Stay away from ponds, child. Avoid stagnant water. Its mirroring could destroy you. You could not withstand seeing what you bear inside. Yours must be an inner vision, not a mere reflection. Stay away from wells. But most of all stay away from *The Lover*. Look how he hesitates, pressed between two women, both staring at him with desire. The young one is beautiful yet he only has eyes for the matron at his right. All he craves for is attention. Cupid hovers over the gallant's head, an arrow ready to escape his tight bow. It is not the right time for you. See, you are linked to life, but only from a distance, viewing it through transparent lenses. Do not expect the gift of life the way you fill empty cups around you. See the woman in *The Star*? Countless stars surround her, reflected in the spring's flowing water, reverberating inside the earthenware. Like her, you will deliver dreams and illusions. Don't worry if yours are not fulfilled. Don't try to be part of other people's lives, share their intimacy. They should preserve their own vessels in a cool, shaded place. You heard that cry because you wanted to be near that child. Remember: a certain closeness is forbidden to you. See the next Arcanum? *The Wheel of Fortune* turns, but what makes it move? Three monkeys racing around each other, the one on top flaunts fleetingly a gilded crown. Your luck may change, but follow their wisdom. Be discreet and patient and you will not be disturbed by the child's cries again."

SUCCESSION

The last snow had melted, life returned to the village with its multitude of sounds. He knew the time had come to leave his wife and son and follow his father's footsteps. He had to know the secret behind his father's disappearance and many others before him. With only a sword, a staff, and some arrows, he penetrated the dense woods.

He thought of his last moments in the village, how he had held his wife in his arms and looked intently at his son. Then, facing the tall white peaks ahead of him, he promised he'd come back before the next snow. The village was situated in a crater surrounded by mountains—the marble mountains no one had ever climbed nor crossed. Legends said they were guarded by packs of white wolves.

Days followed nights and nights followed days for moons and moons and he found no sign of human passage. He dreamed of white wolves and began welcoming them in his sleep. Night after night they regularly haunted him, their baying and howling echoing against the white walls. Waking up anguished, sweating, he found himself alone in the dark with no sign of life, not a single leaf rustling. Snowy shapes followed him at a distance, drifting silently like clouds, until one day, he saw them moving closer and closer.

With time, game became scarce and he wondered how he would survive. Convinced he was the wolves' next prey, he stopped sleeping and built larger and larger fires. For hours, he watched tongues of fire as pallid as the moon spurt and then disappear. How long had it been since he had last felt the warmth of his wife's presence? His beard had grown long and his hair covered his shoulders. In the moonlight he could see silver in his hair, as if moon dust, but the glitter disappeared in daytime.

He became weary of trying to return to the village, paths and trails intersected and resembled each other. He could not be very far, having not left the marble mountains' boundary. Snow had fallen and melted so often that he lost hope of ever finding his father's or any human's trace. He tried to imagine what his son looked like.

There were no more wild animals to hunt. Even the berries, which had sustained him, became scarce. Observing the wolves more closely, he discovered they fed on mice, wild mice that they dug and ate by the hundreds. Desperate, he started eating mice, roasting them on skewers, thankful he was not the next victim. He sensed the wolves wouldn't attack him. Or else why wouldn't they have done it earlier?

His hair was getting grayer; he had abandoned hope of returning home. Only during the long cold vigils, would he dream, eyes wide open, of his wife's body, her slender thighs. But even this memory was fading. Why couldn't he find the way back to the center of the woods, to the crater where he knew his village stood; or had it vanished?

Alone with the wolves and the mice—an endless supply of mice—he doubted his wife was still alive. One day, he came across a clearing. In its midst, a spring flowed over polished stones, coming to rest in a tranquil pool. He knelt, and saw his reflection in the water, touched his long hair, then his beard, strangely surrounding feminine features. But the image disappeared as he got closer to the surface. When he washed his face, and drank from the water, he no longer feared the wolves. In a second, he knew he was losing the memory of his wife, yet he clearly understood what had happened to his father, what was about to happen to his son, as the white wolves surrounded him and his white beard seemed to cover his arms and legs, extending all over his body.

DUCKS' FLIGHT

Mai followed the stranger into a wooded hill overlooking the multitude of whitewashed houses, leaving behind the parched, inhabited valley for the refreshing coolness of ferns and moss-covered paths. Without saying a word, they climbed, turning left, right, until the white geometric shapes waned and disappeared from sight. They were getting deeper into the pine forest, their footsteps crushing dry leaves and pine needles. The scent of mushrooms, wild thyme and mostly resin pervaded the underwoods.

From far away, the mountain looked like a crouched monstrous animal with a dense dark green fur, but as they walked within its flanks, they passed clearings, areas destroyed by fire with dried, blackened trunks, others with stumps sheared as though by a gigantic saw. Then, unexpectedly, patches of dry land with thorny bushes and stones gave way to a thickened vegetation where broken lines of light filtered beneath tall trunks, revealing different shades of green, unmasking lighter tips of growth in all branches, unfurled fern stems, wild vines curling over twisted bark.

She followed him without knowing where they were headed, or what he had in store for her. He wore white cotton pants, a white long sleeved shirt with a high collar and white sneakers. No questions or doubts crossed her mind about the oddness of her situation, nor had she hesitated when she saw him at the village crossroad earlier that day and decided to accompany him into the woods.

Neither had she been surprised the very first time she saw his face—so close, yet so distant, when she was hanging laundry on the terrace's clothes-line. Upon rearranging the alignment of shirts, making sure they were all well stretched and flattened, removing her younger brother's shirt—already dry—she saw his eyes staring at her as surely as if he were next to her, hiding behind the drying sheets. She sensed he was somewhere in the mountain but whenever she'd try to discern his shape within the distant shadows, making a visor of her hands, he'd disappear.

Then she saw him before dusk. She was walking and talking with a group of friends by the village square when suddenly, there he was, looking at her intensely, casually seated on a bench; when she turned around to see him again, the bench was deserted. From then on, his image remained with her. She somehow knew he'd come again, that the two of them were connected in a definite, irrevocable way she could not explain.

She'd accompany the women to the river on laundry days— a chore she had always avoided, pretending she'd be more useful at home. She busied herself while her restless eyes anxiously examined the surrounding foliage. Yet she'd only seen him in the most unexpected places, feeling a gleam of an eye in the darkness, a flicker of motion out of the corner of her eye; as soon as she'd glimpse his presence, he was gone.

Later that day, when she saw him coming out of nowhere on the side of the familiar road, by the foothills, she was returning home, a jug of fresh spring water on the shoulder. She thought he was about to say something, but instead, he smiled and gestured for her to follow him. And now as she walked silently, the cold breeze mixed with smells of resin, mushrooms and wild thyme rushed through her body and lungs. Where were they going? For an instant her skin tightened all over as if alien to her flesh. It was cool up there, a chill overcame her: her knees weakened and she leaned against the soft brown bark. He instantly turned around and held her by the hand. His firm grasp comforted her, dispelling doubts. She could have walked endlessly.

Would they be visible from below? The white flat roofs, so distant now, would be filled with women struggling with billowing sheets, diligently watering flower beds; the men, already back from work, would smoke narguilehs in the verandahs, shaded with vines and bougainvilleas, sipping with absent looks freshly brewed Turkish coffee. Everything was neat and tidy and organized, as was her life until the stranger's eyes invaded her world. She recalled his look; his wavering fawn eyes, never still, like unquiet waters.

She had come to think of him as her elfin prince, the one she had heard about in her childhood, the protean hero of the tales she told her brothers and sisters at nighttime. She feared the white-clothed stranger holding her by the hand was not real. He would disappear at the next turn. She clenched her fist and dug her long nails into his flesh with all her strength. He stopped abruptly and looked at her: a calm, soothing wave rocked her. He was real. She loosened her hand, letting it nest in his palm.

The water jug left under a shade tree, tightly covered with a linen cloth, crossed her mind. She thought of women doing needlework, sewing, kneading elastic dough by the oven's warmth, of children back from school, of the smell of vegetable stews, and the clouds of smoke from skewers crackling over red burning coals rising from patios and terraces beneath white walls. She inhaled the powerful acrid resinous scent, stronger as they entered deeper into the underwoods, concealing every other odor.

Then, the pungency receded as they reached a clearing where a balmy fragrance pervaded and gentle sunrays played with overgrown ferns. He invited her to sit next to him on moss-covered stones and she worried about the way she looked: her hair was uncombed and her dress wrinkled. The light was increasing, suffusing blue patches between the highest pine needles more vividly than with the rising of a new dawn.

Suddenly, she shivered. The light was obscured by a flight of wild ducks—ducks by the thousands, landing all around them. Swarming ducks surrounded them, pushing one another. The moss felt damp and uncomfortable. They looked around only seeing more and more clumsy, unsteady ducks.

A young boy in a white cotton shirt was approaching. It was her younger brother Misha. Without exchanging a word, they walked down the hill in a line, wending their way among greenish-brown backs, avoiding ducks' excrement. The three of them, as in a single movement, swept black, shiny insects off their clothes, arms and legs. Were they coming from the ducks, she wondered? The ground seemed to sway. In the sterile and deserted areas they had crossed on their way up, ducks had sprouted like mushrooms after heavy rains, masking the clearings in a dense, flowing cover, some perching on truncated stumps and dead branches.

What would it be like in the village? She envisioned an invasion of the village's red-tiled roofs and white terraces, ducks dirtying clotheslines, scaring children, taking over the central square's wooden benches, disrupting walkers, destroying gardens and flower beds. Now, the air reeked with a mixture of redolence and wild scents. The sun was setting, its last rays casting orange shades over the dark brown feathers. The stranger led the way, then her brother, then herself.

Mai noticed her brother's white shirt was new with a high collar similar to the stranger's. He also wore white sneakers she had never seen before. She moved quickly towards him to get a closer look. In an effort to avoid webbed feet, her foot caught in a gnarled root. She stumbled and cried out. Alarmed, her brother turned just in time to prevent her from falling, grasping her by the shoulder, offering her his arm to lean on. Her eyes fell over the clearly visible marks on his open palm, the shape of mini crescents. She held him tightly, her knees shaking uncontrollably as he smiled at her with fawn eyes. They were alone at the edge of the valley, the two of them with no sign of the stranger, stepping out of the woods. Misha helped Mai carry the water jug as they walked home over familiar dirt roads towards the homely smell of vegetable stews and grilled meats, away from pine needles and the resinous scent of under wood.

THE MANTIS

She fed on him until he was unable to move or loosen the intricate silky threads encircling him like invisible halos. Enslaved by her desire, she dreamed of his kisses, his skin, his sighs, her inner substance flowed, unraveling through her lips a gossamer clouding his vision, emptying her, converting her into an automaton, a shade, a shell. Her outstretched skin, a palimpsest of all the words said or unsaid, written or conceived, had hardened from so much erasure. She felt it was now thinning, the way stone or marble eroded when rubbed with pumice stone, until it became tattooed inside out in a special script like Sultan Süleyman's talismanic silk caftans entirely woven with verses from the Quran, interspersed with magical numbers.

She wrote unending novels, never sure of a final version, revising constantly, always finding a newer word, a better scene or dialogue. Her characters were not fictitious; she picked them from real life, except none of them was aware of his role. She would always be the lead, chose herself a lover, then eliminate him as easily as if she were Semiramis, the queen of Atlantis or Theodora. Every time she crumpled an unsatisfactory, unwanted page, she felt a kinship with ruthless Jeanne de Navarre, who threw her lovers from the tower of Nesle, discarding them like garbage from a trap leading to the river Seine. Of course her best scenes were erotic, then, there was no need for elaborate dialogue, mere description, recreation of the senses.

But lately, ever since she had a fixation on David, she no longer could distinguish reality from fiction. She had this strange way of looking at him, turning her eyes inside out, mentally reading and rewriting her lines, of course, readjusting the flow of her prose. Trusting, she told him how she operated, leaving the door ajar. But now it was too late. She loved him with all her soul, dearly as ever any human could. And she was not willing to let him go.

He knew the time had come to confront her. He decided it would have to be that same evening at the pub. As they'd sip their usual drinks, he would explain he wasn't ready for a commitment, maybe never would be. He would demand the right to be freed of his role. After all she was weaving a melodramatic saga and he did not feel any affinity with Tristan, neither did he play the harp like the melancholic youth. "You are infringing upon my rights," he said as she drank her Kir Royal. "You have no right to give me parts I did not agree upon, study with care, or properly rehearse." He blew away volutes of smoke, pursing his lips, looking directly into her almond-shaped eyes.

No sooner were these words proffered, than he stood, finishing his second Courvoisier, waiving at the waiter, "*Garçon! L'addition,*" then took out a few bills from his black baby crocodile wallet. He ran his fingers through his long auburn hair repeatedly as if by doing so, he was breaking the silk barrier, grown so tight it paralyzed his movements, even controlled his dreams from a distance. Tearing the cocoon he was being buried alive in, he burst out. For a minute that lasted forever, he remained still, unsure of his steps the way one does upon recovering from a long illness.

"How easy," she thought. "He set me apart with one look, swirls of pestilential Gitanes, as if I were a vulgar Aphid. I was no longer *persona grata* in his private orchard. How simple. He did not need to erect gilded gates or post signs forbidding my entrance, he did not need to grow sinewy bindweed all over fences, all over wrought iron doors and windows, silencing the softest breeze, so that he might find peace. Should I not long anymore for the scent of fresh lilacs he'd steal for me at night from neighboring gardens? Should I forget my hopes of visiting Florence with him and eat *gelato* together along the Ponte Vecchio? Should I forget our first trip to Rome, our senses in rapture as we watched *Aida*, holding hands at the Thermae of Caracalla? And what of our plans to go down the Nile next Christmas, to Upper Egypt?" She could no longer recall what he had said a while ago. She wondered if there were no one to hear, would sound exist? And if there were no one to love, would love exist?

"But love, that fleeting illusion, branding one with letters of fire, is fragile, even for a Mantis, or even a mutant Mantis wanting to emulate a Tarantula," she could hear herself think. A few words, a look, and all the inscriptions, the love words engraved inside her vanished into air, blown by the wind, disappearing like invisible ink. "I will never be able to write again," she thought, feeling pain in her chest. And now that he could breathe freely, now that his tall, elegant silhouette was disappearing through the pub's revolving door, she was left without her protagonist.

Then Vlado suddenly appeared, walking down from the upper level billiard room. He came straight to her with a smile: "I've tried calling you several times. You're never home or what?"

She looked at the twenty-six-year-old Slavic reporter. He definitely had deep, velvety eyes. "I know now why Irene was crazy about him," she suddenly realized.

"I just came back from Indonesia, you know. I can't wait to show you my pictures. They're really great, rice fields, sampans, floating gardens . . . the most spectacular sunsets. What about dinner tonight? I have a surprise for you but I'll keep it for later, much later. . . . You'll like it, trust me."

She had been to his apartment before. It was at the rooftop of a building with a bird's eye view of Paris' seizième. She could hardly speak, hurting as if thousands of pumice stones were at work, scraping her, cleaning each and every pore inside out.

"I don't feel up to it, Vlado. Maybe some other time."

Ignoring her, he loudly ordered a beer, "*Garçon! Une Stella, s'il vous plaît,*" and "What will *you* have?" he asked, as he kept talking, and talking, certain he'd convince her.

"The same," she nodded and stared at his engaging, insisting smile. She took a deep breath, looked at him straight in the eyes, and said: "It's OK for tonight." "Why not?" she asked herself. She'd be the prey for a change. She was tired of chasing elusive butterflies. She and Vlado will cast the parts together. She began to formulate her opening lines. The next novel will not be about love. No. There will be a mystery, solved by teamwork. She would not use real characters, ever again. It was not good for her writing.

THE FLOOD

She was surrounded by women covered from head to toe with bright colored silks emerging from the rising waters, looking awry while sliding their long veil over their hair with slender hands, revealing their breasts the way petals open up to show hidden pistils, she worried when similar figures began sprouting from the torrents like mushrooms after heavy rain in every corner of the woods, all seemed to float like celluloid dolls seated cross legged, and staring intensely at her as they flaunted their nakedness while she was surprised she could still walk in the midst of the flood, the waters not so deep then, she thought, when something terrible happened she was unable to remember, except seeing herself clinging to him, her savior, along with the faint image of a couple resting on a bench under a double row of poplars in an avenue spared from the torrent and although she struggled, she couldn't recollect what she had just escaped from right after facing that strange look given to her by the series of budding women, a spectacle orchestrated with special effects, she tried harder but couldn't visualize what had followed, but it doesn't matter she thought, since he had witnessed it all and would help her reconstruct the scene, too bad she didn't record in writing the last part of her dream just before finding herself on the bench next to him, with so much energy flowing between the two of them, there was no doubt he had rescued her when she was running away from these apparitions only to experience this something that has been erased from her memory for no apparent reason, but not from his own consciousness of course, she could tell because he understood her, oh so well, and it is overwhelmed with emotion that she leaned towards him convinced he was feeling the same way, such an intensity never felt before when they kissed in the car, she, giving out her whole self in that long kiss, losing track of time since he was the one who pulled away from her, we've arrived he said in an indistinct, hoarse voice, as if feeling guilty, she should understand his position he explained right away, not that he didn't care but he couldn't do otherwise, and as he spoke she found herself in an office surrounded by several men and women, especially a young blonde girl doting on him while he was acting as if nothing had ever happened between the two of them, despite realizing she'd been going through a whirlwind, had escaped the deluge, after being harassed by these strange women, how could he not be aware of that horrible black hole, leaving her with this unbearable void, seeing him so indifferent just when she thought their passion was real, explosive, when they were about to become one, forget everything else, step into another reality, he acted so formal, as if they were only what they had always been for years, just friends, since this was merely one of the many dreams in which she'd assign him a role, maybe all leading to this dream, the most powerful she'd ever had, and now she would never know, since she couldn't remember its crucial parts, it would take a very long time to get over it, and to think she was counting on him to tell her what he had undoubtedly witnessed, to find herself confronted with this loss, unable to understand the reason for her despair, since she kept telling herself it was only a dream.

SHUFFLING SEASONS

It hailed white sand over oak leaves carpeting the woods. Abstracted, Lisa watched the brown curls lighten up rapidly with the relentless pouring, hoping the tiny ice particles would not disappear, that logs, twigs, bushes and branches would retain their crisp, unexpected look.

It was as though hours refused to pass, a backwards transition into winter, an instantaneous stretch in time. She walked through the long narrow corridor, a slender silhouette pacing the marble floor, looking out the vast bay windows, waiting for something, for someone she knew would never come. By noon, no sign was left of the morning's elusive vision.

At sunset, she lit the crystal chandeliers as though she was expecting company. She then took the blue irises that she had hurriedly placed in a bucket the day before, and arranged them in a tall Lalique vase, one by one. Satisfied, she curled up in the corner of the den, the only room she allowed to remain in darkness in contrast with the rest of the lighted house. Releasing her coiled hair, she gathered it on one side, combing it with her fingers, weaving and unweaving a single long braid.

Longing for sunshine when it snowed, and for brisk, cool wind in August, she withdrew into a world where successive time ceased to affect her. Or was she trying to refute its irrevocability? Seeing Tony was at the tip of her fingertips, as close as the phone next to her. Lisa reached for the smooth, cold receiver, covering it with her cupped hand, and thought of feeling again the closeness of his chest and arms.

Outside, intermittent green lights transmitted a secret code: fireflies, stars of grass, so early, so numerous this year. She thought of long summer nights, of a child chasing fugitive stars, bringing home her prize, only to discover in the morning a helpless bug in a glass jar.

Her hours were a succession of weary dawns, hopes and dreams, unified by a same yearning. She'd close her eyes, think of him and see the flicker of an oil lamp, an evanescent light that disappeared when she opened her eyes, fragile flame she kept burning next to an indifferent icon.

Images shifted in her mind, succeeding one another, precious photographs rescued from dismantled albums. Through past and present losses, her selective memory accompanied and defined her, weaving harmoniously the disparities of her life.

Covering her closed eyes, as one does from the blazing sun, she gently rubbed her eyelids. Fires ravaging rain forests im-posed themselves on her mind. Terror-stricken multitudes of thumping hoofs, outstretched wings and agile paws appeared, fleeing faster than raging wind, yet seemingly motionless through the dense smoke. Flames would disappear for a while, converted into embers, vanishing though burning under-ground. Soon, sparks would ignite again, rise as if from nowhere in gigantic bonfires, crackling high in constant renewal, then fading away into a desolate, cold hearth.

She imagined what Tony would say, what she yearned to say, all her expectations wavering, rekindled by every trembling of the mutable flame. He had not gotten over a painful separation, and was eager to preserve his freedom. They had agreed on a non-committal relationship. In theory, that is, because she could not handle the situation, nor could she give him up. The memory of their kisses, insubstantial, took another dimension as she sensed the gentle warmth of the receiver in her moist palm.

Would he come for an hour, or two, maybe? Maybe not. She envisioned a deserted, silent stage, the two of them, each a garment to one another's nakedness, feeling the purity of going back into the original funnel, rediscovering the primal closeness of one's own conception.

Then, holding the door open, she would once again see his back, want to run her fingers through the curls nesting in the nape of his neck. It might as well not have happened. It was only an image as other images, part of the collection of photographs she mentally shuffled at random.

With difficulty, she slowly detached the receiver from her hand, carefully replaced it on its cold stand and watched the fireflies. Against the windowpanes, green lights were pressing themselves in greater numbers. Soon, very soon, it would be summer again.

FLIGHT

It all happened when she swallowed the sparrow. Or was it a hummingbird? She vaguely remembered. At any rate it was dark that night and the bird so tiny. It entered her mouth while she was eating soup by the hearth and vanished into her belly, evanescent. At first, she doubted anything had happened and thought of his disbelief when she'd tell him. But many sunrises and sunsets would rhythmically encompass her tilling and weaving until she'd see him again.

She had lived with him for so many years, she reflected, comfortably reclining on a pillow, eyes fixed on the crackling embers, had loved him through shattered hopes and dreams. With no children to care for, nor to keep her company, her love resisted the flow of life. She waited patiently for his return from long journeys in the mountain peaks, silently watching the simmering copper pot that hung from an iron hook above the glowing coals. She loved him with her many faces, with the several skins she shed unwillingly over the years.

Carefully lifting a long wooden ladle to her mouth, she inhaled the warm vapor, and sipped the soup, adding more ingredients day after day: fresh or dried vegetables, spices and herbs, a piece of meat at times. That day, she threw a handful of chick peas in the concoction which never tasted quite the same yet retained a continuity, harmoniously tying their life together.

But ever since she swallowed the bird, she turned and tossed in her sleep, dreaming of the trapped shape, growing, fluttering inside her. She'd sense shiny beaded eyes searching for a way out, staring at her in the utmost darkness. With time, she grew accustomed to this presence taking over her nights, to the raging pulse from within forcing her to clasp her pillow in a desperate attempt to anchor herself.

In the mornings, she'd check her waist. Her stomach seemed to curve a little. Seated on her favorite pillow, she'd weave fine threads of colored wool, weave incessantly, recreating in a rug that never seemed the same, the emerald, turquoise and silver feathers of her dreams. She gradually developed an uncontrollable appetite as the bird fed on the soup, and her dreams became nightmares in which beaks tore her apart, stabbing her flesh, forcing her to change position during her deepest sleep. She imagined huge, powerful wings stretching, unfolding, opening her like a clam. Sweating, she'd wake up, unable to sleep again, feeling her tender belly.

The time came when she realized she could not hide this increasing swelling from the people in the village. What would he say when he'd return from his long absence? If only he'd been here to share her dreams and nightmares! She'd talk in her sleep—and waking—to the bird, but now, the discomfort would not disappear in the mornings. She then knew she had to consult the Old Man.

"Words, my child. . . . You won't regret to pay me for the words that I will say. Words can heal, but can also pierce your heart. Words, my child, are at the root of your suffering. Words like blades' edges, sharpened knives, obsidian daggers . . . words transform feathers into steel and silex. The bird is made of words you keep buried, words that do not belong to you, that need to go to their master.

"Go! Build a pyre on the highest point of this slope, on the side where the sun rises. Mix a few locks of your hair with these herbs and this twig thrice dipped in the blood of sacrificial animals. While you watch them turn to ashes, talk, talk until you have no more to say and the weight will disappear, soaring where it belongs. These are my words, my child."

That night, she did not fight the bird, she did not toss around. In her dream, she saw herself flying above a shadow, towards a nest on top of the highest mountain still covered with snow. But her body was protecting the flight of a hummingbird of unusual proportions. She watched it get stronger, bigger, spread voluminous wings and stretch a white-feathered neck, until they reached the condor's nest.

When she woke up, her waist was slender again and her curves had regained their natural shape. She added a handful of black beans to the copper pot, stirred the mixture, rekindled the fire, and resumed her weaving, attentive to the flickering cinders. At sunset, she quietly lay on her favorite pillow and closed her eyes. She felt his lips pressed against hers and his strong arms around her. Through her half-closed eyes, she noticed his hair was forming a silver crown around his neck and his cape was enveloping like wings.